The Cat Lady by the Sea

Jeannie A. Langston

PublishAmerica
Baltimore

First printing

At the specific preference of the author, PublishAmerica allowed this work to remain exactly as the author intended, verbatim, without editorial input.

ISBN: 1-4241-6205-X
PUBLISHED BY PUBLISHAMERICA, LLLP
www.publishamerica.com
Baltimore

Printed in the United States of America

Dedication

I dedicate this book to my mother Alice Day Coon who although she has gone on to be with the Lord, made her dream come true when she became the Cat Lady by the Sea. Your unconditional love has always given me wings and helped me to believe in myself.

I will always hold you in my heart. I miss you, Momma.

Acknowledgment

I would like to thank my dear friends Barbara Godfrey and Jamie Underwood who encouraged me and listened to my ideas and were voices of faith during my times of doubt.

I'd also like to thank the man of my heart, my husband Jimmy. He's been my partner in love and life and the one who has stood by my side through it all and made my life more abundant.

Chapter One

She knew that she should have put some real clothes on. Pajama's are cute and cover all your limbs but hardly appropriate when trying to flag down someone for help. She had just thrown a jacket on over her Tweety Bird pajamas and thought to herself, *I'll be back in ten minutes. My pajamas cover more than some of my everyday clothes do, I'll be fine. I have no reason to feel self conscious.*

It seemed like such a quick simple trip. She had a terrible craving for chocolate and she thought she'd just ride over to the Ice Cream Shoppe and go through the drive through. They had the best hot fudge cake that she had ever tasted. But for some reason even the best laid plans can be thwarted.

For some reason she couldn't quite understand, her sweet little car had coughed and spitted and then stopped. So unfortunately, she found herself sitting in her yellow Volkswagen Beetle on the side of the road, wearing her Tweety Bird pajamas and her pink bunny slippers, eating a hot fudge cake and holding a frightened Siamese cat named Lancelot who thought he was a prince. Melanie Byron was in a pickle.

She had wanted to make a good impression on her new neighbors. *Maybe they don't know me well enough to recognize me yet*, she thought. *They might think I'm a little odd if they see me like this.*

Lancelot was mortified. To Melanie it was pretty obvious. He had always thought that he should be owned by nobility or even the elite wealthy but instead he ended up with her. She had known he was a special cat from the moment she saw him at the pound and she knew the moment she laid eyes on him that she had to rescue him. Lance had held himself so proudly even during the humiliating process of being ogled by prospective owners at the pound. He was grateful that Melanie had taken him in, although he'd never show it. So he endured her unorthodox ways and loved her anyway. He couldn't help it if he was a little regal, it's just who he is.

Melanie had bought the vintage Volkswagen Beetle for the convertible top and the yellow paint. She hadn't really thought about the motor very much. The minute she saw Old Yeller beside the Feed and Seed store back home, she knew that she had to have her. She wondered if she had actually heard the car call her name. Well maybe not, but she certainly felt a connection. She hoped the yellow paint wasn't a sign that Old Yeller was going to be a lemon.

Melanie made up her mind right away that a convertible was the best way to enjoy the scenery. The scenery from West Virginia to the North Carolina coast was wonderful. How awesome God's creation is. She didn't know any mechanics in Long Beach and she didn't have one single person that she could call. Well on second thought, she did have one friend that most people would consider to be in pretty high places.

"Well Lord, it's me again Melanie and I'm calling on you, I need some intervention here. Could you send some really nice neighborly person who likes cats to take us home? We'll just sit here and wait. Thanks Lord for coming to my rescue once again."

It seemed like such a good idea for Melanie to move to the coast of North Carolina and fulfill her dream of opening her own pet shop. The yellow VW was the icing on the cake. The icing might be melting right now but the cake could still be tasty. This town seemed so friendly when she came to check it out, that she decided right away to move here. Leaving her past behind was the primary reason for relocating but the advertisement of a store front shop for rent didn't hurt either. Her dream of running her own pet shop was becoming reality and this little setback couldn't stop her, she had come too far to turn back now.

She knew she shouldn't let herself be too stressed out by this situation so she took a minute to be thankful for all she had and she breathed a "prayer" of thanks. *This is really me, none other than Melanie Byron, who has a new house near the beach and a new pet shop opening in a few days and a new church that doesn't know about my brother. Life is good. I am escaping my past. Thank you Lord.*

Melanie considered herself a regular twenty-seven-year-old woman. Not too tall not too short. Her hair was curly, long and brown, her eyes were also brown and very expressive and most importantly her heart was set on living for God. She was not skinny but not fat either. She enjoyed the fact that she could eat hot fudge cakes occasionally and not gain much weight. So what if she did get fat? It didn't really matter because God looked at the inside and he was the one who really counted. She certainly didn't want to get any male attention. She knew that she could be attractive if she worked at it but she was happy with herself and that was what mattered. Her family had taken up most of her time and energy for the past couple of years but thank God that chapter of her life had been left far behind her. It was time to get started living her new life.

Having been shunned by most of the people in her hometown, she had a real fear of trusting anyone again. If the friends and neighbors who had known her all her life could turn on her, how could she ever believe that anyone could be trusted to stand by her when times got tough? Her father hadn't been there for her for most of her life and her mother and her brother had deserted her too. Even if they had no control over leaving, she still felt the pain of rejection. The relationship that she had developed with God had helped fill the void that she felt inside. She could get involved in God's work as long as she didn't put too mush faith in his people. The church family that she had known back home had turned on her too. She had learned about how fickle human nature could be. Even though she had been hurt, she would never let that keep her from going to church.

Pastor Grey back home had been kind enough to give her the name of a church to try in Long Beach. He just happened to have a really good Pastor friend who oversaw a church here. His friend's name was Anthony Goodwin and he had turned out to be a wonderful Bible teacher. A few weeks ago when Melanie walked into his church it had felt like coming home. She absolutely loved it. God is so good.

They had incredible worship and such a strong children and youth program. She had been teaching children's Sunday School for the past five years. She had prayed about it and hoped that a door would open for her to be involved with the children at her new church. Pastor Grey had already put in a good word for her with her new Pastor.

Melanie decided to get out of the car and open the hood. Even though it was dark, there was a possibility that someone might see her and not be too frightened by her appearance to stop. She popped the hood which was actually in the trunk and peeked inside. She hoped that the friendly passerby that the Lord sent to help her knew that the trunk was actually the hood in a vintage VW Beetle. The Tweety Bird pajamas were not frightening just kind of cute, or so she thought when she bought them.

Melanie liked to annoy Lance (the cat) and the large yellow bird on her pajamas did freak him out at first. He finally decided that he would tolerate it and snuggled down beside her and looked bored. Looking bored was what he did best. He had it down to a science. Melanie was hoping that eventually he would develop a sense of humor. So far he hasn't shown any signs of one.

The floppy eared bunny slippers were a trial to Newman, her other cat, because the bunnies on them are so big that they were almost life sized and he wanted to chase them around the house. Newman showed up on Melanie's doorstep one day looking half starved. He's a big orange tabby who appeared to have lived a hard life before he came to her. He seemed unfortunately not be too bright. His right ear was torn into two flaps and this tended to give him a roguish appearance. But he had such a sweet disposition that even

Lance liked him although he wouldn't let anyone see him act like it. He did get a little wacky when he saw those slippers. Maybe he dreamed of being a rabbit cat or something. After the first thirty minutes, Newman finally wore himself out from chasing those pesky rabbits and just sat in the corner and kept an eye on them. If Melanie left them in the floor, so he could reach them, he would attack them and have long intense battles fighting them off in the middle of the night. This could be annoying so the bunnies were kept on the closet shelf.

Newman, Lance and Pepe' the Chihuahua were Melanie's family. They were like children to her. Her long term plan was to have a great life without having children. She would dearly love to have children but in order to have them she would have to have a husband. She certainly didn't want one of those. She pictured herself as a woman of God who would be a cat lady that lived by the sea. Technically the sea was two blocks over from her little house but she could walk to the sea and that was good enough for her.

Pepe' had an identity crisis. He thought he was a large dog. He was a little brown bundle of energy that weighed all of three pounds. If he needed to be taller he jumped. When Melanie walked into the house, if he wanted her to pet him, he jumped up and down beside her so that she couldn't ignore him. When they went for a walk, he did not hesitate to bark and growl at large dogs. He ignored small dogs like he didn't think they were worth his notice. He'd walk up and start a hello sniff with a German Shepard in a flash. That was why he had to be watched constantly. He got himself into trouble on a regular basis. Melanie had to actually take him out of a Great Dane's mouth once. She suspected that Queen (the Great Dane) had just been playing with him, but then again, Queen might have had a stray thought of what a little dog of Hispanic descent might taste like

Michael Logan was driving home from work on that particular night with feeling discontented with his life. He was a man of deep faith that was getting impatient with God. He had been praying and expecting to meet his helpmate for years now and so far he'd seen no sign of her. His life was full with his work, the youth at church and taking care of his widowed mother, but he yearned for more. His heart's desire was to have a woman to love and children. Not just any woman but the woman that God had for him. Michael saw the silly little car beside the road and slowed down. He saw the beautiful woman with the silly clothes and he felt a jolt of recognition. Could this strange woman holding a cat be the one he'd been waiting for?

Melanie looked and realized that here appeared to be a large green pickup truck coming up behind old yeller and slowing down. It looked like a single man alone in the truck. He was a big man. Not just tall big but his muscles were big. Big men scared Melanie. One thing she remembered about her father was that he had been a big man. She couldn't really remember him being kind. She did vaguely remember that he and her mother had yelled at each other a lot. Her mother had told her many times that most men couldn't be trusted. This was not what the Bible taught but her mother's words were running through Melanie's head. She tried her best to silence her frightened thoughts. *"Lord, is this my friendly neighbor person?"*

Michael had no idea that he was having such an effect on the pretty lady. He was a large man standing six feet four inches and weighing two hundred and twenty five pounds. He didn't have an ounce of fat on him because of the hard physical labor of his job. He worked as a General Contractor helping to rebuild and restore some of the homes on the coast that had been damaged by storms. Some folks most likely would consider him a good old boy. He was in fact as gentle as a kitten and certainly not the type of man who would intentionally scare a woman.

The large man was getting out of his truck and walking Melanie's way. Her heart was racing. Fear was the opposite of faith so she swallowed her fear and decided that she would believe that this was a nice neighborly man that would help her, and not a large scary man who would hurt her. She realized that she really should have been more specific in her prayer and asked for a grandfatherly neighbor person. The big man was walking right up to the car. His face did look kind. In fact his face looked like he was trying not to laugh. This did not bode well for future friendship. He'd better not mention anything about Melanie's Tweedy Bird pajamas and bunny slippers.

On closer inspection he was really kind of handsome. His jaw was square and strong. His face was kind of round with apples in his cheeks and a dimple in his chin. His green eyes were twinkling with mirth right that minute. He had short cropped dark hair. His muscular build reminded Melanie of a bulldog strong and stocky. If he were a bulldog he'd be a handsome loveable bulldog. She'd always heard that eyes were the window of the soul. His eyes looked soft and kind and reminded her of the sea. Her racing pulse slowed in relief when she realized that this was not a dangerous man. Melanie hated to admit it but she was especially fond of bulldogs. That didn't mean she'd be interested in this guy. She certainly didn't want a man in her life messing up all her wonderful plans.

"Are you having trouble, Miss? I'd be glad to help if I can."

This sounded like her chance to practice being sweet and humble so she just swallowed her pride and asked; "Could you possibly give us a lift? We only live down on Fifty-Second Street. My name is Melanie Byron. I could call somebody to come and see about the car tomorrow."

"Who is with you, or are you referring to the big yellow bird on your shirt?" This was said with just enough mirth to irritate her but now was not the time to develop a bad attitude. She pulled the cat out of the car and tried to look sheepish.

"A cat.," He said in a surprised tone of voice, "Let me get this straight. You are driving a bright yellow car, wearing a large yellow bird and cruising around with a cat? Lady you certainly could make life a little more interesting around here." He was obviously looking at her hand to see if she had a wedding ring.

Melanie didn't expect that there would be many people who'd be too thrilled about giving a snobby cat a ride home but she couldn't leave him there. Lance was not just a cat he was family and she would never leave him there alone. He was already upset and he needed to be home in his own bed.

The big man stuck out his hand and said, "Hi, I'm Michael Logan. I'd be glad to give you and your cat a ride home. The poor guy doesn't look too happy to be here." Well, Melanie thought, what a surprise, a big man who actually noticed that her cat looked unhappy. This made her feel so much better about accepting a ride. "*Thank you Lord.*"

"This is Lance and he very seldom looks happy. If a ride out for ice cream doesn't make you happy, I'm not sure what would work. We would appreciate a ride very much."

"You and Lance hop in and I'll have you home in a few short minutes." Melanie got into the truck and began to pray under her breath. "*Lord get us home safe, please and let Michael be a nice guy with a wife and kids.*" The way he kept looking over and grinning at her and Lance, she got a funny feeling that this man might be single. This was not something she would want to encourage.

His truck was not very clean and had tools and various items laying in the seat and floorboard. She thought he must be in some kind of construction but she didn't ask. She wouldn't want to appear interested in him.

"My family just moved here and we haven't found a dependable garage yet. Do you know someone who we could call?" *Lord, I'm not lying I just don't want him to think I'm available. He doesn't have to know that my family is two cats and a dog.*

Michael looked at her with those twinkling green eyes and replied, "There's a friend of mine from church who has a garage out on the highway. I'll write his number down for you." He seemed to be trying to put her at ease and it was working. *He goes to church, this is wonderful.* Thoughts swirled in her head. *I am so glad this nice man stopped to help me. I should be more grateful and stop worrying about it if he looks my way. I can be friendly and appreciate his kindness. It's not like I'm likely to ever see him again. I have to keep telling myself to stop being so suspicious of men but I'll have to admit this is a test of my paranoia for sure.* God did send him Melanie decided.

"Thank you so much for stopping and helping us. I would appreciate getting your friend's number. Does he have a tow truck?"

"Sure John can fix you up. He's the best mechanic around these parts. He won't take advantage of you."

"Do you think just because I'm a woman I can be taken advantage of by a male mechanic? That is a chauvinistic remark."

"Anybody can be taken advantage of by a dishonest mechanic. Not just females, boy are you touchy." He was approaching the turn off to her house and she quietly told him the address.

"You can turn right at this next intersection. The house number is 3511." He made the turn and slowed to a crawl as he looked for the house number.

"It's the next to the last house on the right."

Melanie was so proud of her little house two blocks over from the sea. It was small but had lots of character. It had an open floor plan with living space below and a loft bedroom space above. She positioned her bed just right so that she could lie in bed and see the ocean in the distance. The exterior siding was a little weathered but showed character. The tree lined front yard required little mowing because of the pine needles, but still got enough sun for shrubs and flowers. The yard was a work in progress but she could see it in her mind the way it could be. Michael might see her house as a little shabby, but who cared what he thought. It was her dream sea cottage and she loved it. She was not trying to impress anyone.

She saw Newman in the window waiting and it felt like home. Michael pulled in the driveway and she quickly reached for the door handle. "Thank you for coming to our rescue. You are a good Samaritan."

"You are most welcome. Maybe I'll see you around." She knew that she was not being kind but her first thought was, *Not very likely if I can help it.* But she tried to be nice. "Yeah I'm here to stay. Thanks again."

After getting back into the house she thought about it and realized how God had taken care of her in that situation. Someone who could have intended her harm might have stopped. Michael Logan might have been scared her a little at first, but he had a kind heart. Melanie reminded herself that she had to stop being paranoid about strangers, especially male strangers. Her past might be behind her in West Virginia but she still had some reactions associated with it that she needed to work on. She knew that she really should get her Bible out and look up some verses on fear. She just couldn't seem to muster up the energy tonight. *I'll do it tomorrow; I'm so tired*; she tells herself. *"Lord, please help me to overcome my unnatural reactions to men. Lord please show me how to forget those things behind and push towards the mark."*

The next day was another beautiful sunny warm day for February and Melanie decided to walk down to the beach. A little cold couldn't stop her from enjoying the fact that up until a couple of weeks ago she would have had to drive for hours and hours to see the ocean. Now all she had to do was walk out her front door. She decided to take Pepe' her little dog with her this morning. She figured that Lance would prefer to stay at home for a while after his ordeal last night. It was too early to call the mechanic and she was not going to worry about it. She just wanted to enjoy the beauty of God's creation in the early morning hours. *"Early will I seek thee Lord."*

Just a few minutes alone with God in the mornings made the day so much better. Everyone needed to have time to get the trials of life into perspective. Even though Melanie had a car broken down on the side of the road she was at peace this morning. She didn't have to go to the pet shop today since it hadn't opened yet and the beach was calling her name. Life is good.

As she started to walk along Fifty-Second Street, something caught her eye. It appeared to be a strange older looking lady in the yard next door. She was sitting in a lawn chair out in her front yard with a large floppy hat on her head. Now floppy hats were nice on some people but there appeared to be some type of small stuffed animal on top of her hat and Melanie didn't seem to be able to help herself, she stared at her. Something must have caught the lady's attention because she looked Melanie's way and smiled. Melanie, not being a person to pass up an opportunity to investigate further, went over and struck up a conversation just to get a better look. At closer scrutiny it looked like a possible muskrat.

"Hi, I'm Melanie your new neighbor. I was just admiring your unusual hat." Well if she didn't want a conversation starter she wouldn't wear rodents on her head.

"Hello dear, I'm Helen it's nice to meet you. It's also very nice of you to mention liking my hat. Most people just talk about my hats behind my back and make fun of me. I have a philosophy about hats. Hats are happy and they make me smile. They can also make other people smile so I'm spreading joy. Behind my back the children call me the Mad Hat Lady. That's really fine because I know who I am in Christ and I don't need the approval of man."

Melanie knew in her heart from that very moment that she wanted Helen for a friend. She might be an elderly lady but she has real style on the inside where it counted. "It's so nice to meet you Helen. My dog Pepe' and I were just enjoying the beauty of God's creation and taking a walk over to the beach. I would like to get better acquainted with you though. How would you like to come over for coffee later?"

Helen turned out to be quite an interesting lady and not just because she wore outrageous hats. She had traveled around the world with her husband, George. She had been to all the foreign places that most people only dreamed about. She also was a strong woman of faith. She had lost her husband fifteen years ago to a long illness. Her only son had died in a car accident just three years ago. She was having a hard time finding any hope in her life when she found a much deeper relationship with God. She found comfort and wisdom in his word. She was a survivor and Melanie felt so fortunate to have her for a new friend. She also loved animals and had a Cocker Spaniel named Peaches. Melanie hadn't met Peaches yet but she sounded like a really sweet companion for Helen.

Having lost her mother just a couple of years ago, Melanie could relate to Helen's pain. Melanie's own mother had passed away from lung cancer. There were times that Melanie wanted to be angry at her for being so careless with her health. It shouldn't have come as such a surprise because she had smoked since she was a young girl. It was a sad way to die but she had made her peace with God at the end. Melanie thanked the Lord for that. She knew that the experience had changed her life in many ways. She had often told friends, "If anybody ever tells you they know how you feel when you loose someone close to you, don't believe it unless they have experienced it for themselves." The loss had been devastating for her and her brother Jerry. That was one of the things that had pushed him to move to the city. He wanted to get away from the pain but he found trouble instead.

They had been the outcasts of their little town for a long time. They were known as the kids with the hand me down clothes and the runaway father, the strange Byron kids who had spent more time with animals than people. Even with the stigma of being outsiders in their community they had always belonged there until the trouble had come that turned the town against them. Well that painful time was behind Melanie now. She was living her new life.

The Cat Lady had now met the Hat Lady. Things were most certainly getting interesting for Melanie. She just had a couple of minor setbacks to deal with. There was the broken down car, and the shipment of birds that were late for the shop, and of course the only brother that she had who was spending the next fifteen years in prison.

Chapter Two

Melanie's family was beyond dysfunctional. Her father left them when Jerry was two and she was four. Their mother had told them repeatedly that he had gotten tired of being a family man and wanted his freedom. All she knew for sure was that she never heard from him again after he left, until last year during Jerry's troubles.

The stigma of having a father who left is hard to overcome for a child. Especially in a small town where everyone knows each other's life history and family tree for three generations. Her little family had been branded as white trash almost from the moment they came to town. Rumors had run wild and her mother never bothered to correct any misconceptions. They all thought that her mother had many affairs and that her father was a mean alcoholic that beat the children.

Melanie doesn't remember being mistreated by her father. She was also pretty sure that her mother didn't see other men. Her mother didn't have anything good to say about any man since her husband had left. Everything that had ever happened to her, she seemed to be able to trace back to some man who was not to be trusted. Melanie really didn't know why her parents divorced. The information that she got from her mother made it seem that it was all her father's fault. He did come to town during the trial. That was more than anyone else had done for them.

He came to Melanie's house in West Virginia and tried to tell her a bunch of lies about how their mother thrown him out and took his children away so he that he couldn't find them. The truth was that they had moved after he left because they couldn't afford the house anymore. Their Momma had family in West Virginia. Her sister Rose lived there and she had offered to help her get a job working in a shirt factory. The cost of living was much cheaper there too.

Melanie always believed in her heart that her father could have found them if he had tried. Her mother's family knew where they were. She remembers sitting by the window as a little girl making up stories in her head about her dream father. He would love her and spend time with her and never scream or throw things. He would always be there when she needed him and would never let anyone make fun of her again. She did finally find her dream father in God. He's the only father that she ever had, and she doesn't feel she needs the earthly one now after all these years.

Melanie soon found out that animals could be depended on more than people. Animals would always love you no matter what you have or where you live. She'd always had pets since she was a little girl. She and Jerry would play in the woods and make friends with all kinds of animals. Melanie could even approach some wild animals. She had a rare gift with them. There were always animals around their house that she had brought home. They even had a pet deer for a while. They had found him after his mother and been killed by a hunter. Jerry and Melanie had allowed him his freedom to roam loose in the woods but they fed him and he trusted them. When the deer got bigger and grew a large rack of horns, they had to relocate him for his own safety. He trusted men and men are not to be trusted, especially by a large buck with a nice rack of horns. Jerry and Melanie spent all their spare time outside with the animals. Those were magic times for them. Melanie will always treasure those memories with her brother. They had shared a closeness that was more intense than the relationship between most siblings.

Melanie's gift with animals had become a sort of side job for her back home. She worked as an unofficial veterinary assistant, when she wasn't working at the Feed and Seed. When the people didn't have the money to call in the vet from the city, they would call her. She had learned some of the old mountain remedies for simple illnesses. If anyone found a wild animal that was hurt, they would bring it to her and she would do her best to nurse it back to health.

She had always dreamed of owning a pet shop. To get the right pets together with the right owner could be so rewarding. Melanie had gotten a taste of how much she loved it while working at the Feed and Seed. They carried some puppies and kittens and a few fish. It was like the general store for animals and farmers. There were some magic times when someone would be looking for an animal and she was able to find them just the right one. To a farmer who had to replace a working dog that had been a vital part of his family and farm, choosing an intelligent pup with the right herding instincts was a major decision. Melanie had the gift of knowing how to match up pets and owners. She had proved her instincts to be reliable many times back home.

She didn't just rely on her way with animals to insure the success of her shop. She had gotten her degree in business administration via an online college program. She wasn't foolish enough to think that she could run a business without a sound business plan. She worked two jobs along with taking in an occasional animal patient to get the money squirreled away while she took classes, to fulfill her dream of having a pet shop. She had come too far to turn back now. She just needed to come up with a clever attention grabbing name. Melanie's Pet Shop was so boring. She considered something to do with Noah's Ark like Melanie's Ark but decided against it. She really wanted to come up with something soon so that the sign could be made in time for the grand opening. She decided she would just have to pray and it would most likely come to her. It had to be perfect.

By Sunday Melanie had her life back in order. Her car was fixed and the problem turned out to be a minor one, and the missing bird shipment had come in. Unfortunately the guest bedroom in her new house was going to temporarily be filled with parakeets and hamsters and gerbils. She also had a small snake in the utility room. The temporary house guests in the bedroom had already made Newman act a little bonkers; she didn't know how he'd handle a new snake.

Lancelot sniffed around for a few minutes and went back to looking bored. He seemed to have recovered from his ordeal. He didn't seem very interested in riding in the car yet though. Melanie was a little worried that the neighbors might hear strange noises coming from the house and wonder about her, if they haven't already. She had wanted to make a good impression but, oh well; she has to be who she is. God made her this way.

The church parking lot looked really crowded that morning as Melanie pulled in and found a place to park. Someone might have mentioned something about it being youth Sunday but she wasn't sure what that entailed. Well anything that gets the kids involved couldn't be too bad.

As she walked toward the front door she heard some unusual music coming from inside the church. This might be interesting. A group of teens were on the podium playing instruments and singing. Some of the teens in the front of the church had their hands raised and their eyes closed. They were praising God. It was a sobering sight for Melanie. If only she could have gotten her brother Jerry to take an interest in God as a teen, his life could have turned out so much differently. Tears came into her eyes as she thought of Jerry's wasted life. She was determined that his mistakes wouldn't ruin her life too. She decided to join in and praise God with the kids. Melanie Byron certainly had a lot to be thankful for.

As the music faded and it was time for the sermon, Melanie saw a large man making his way to the podium. She found herself having to do a double take. It couldn't possibly be Michael Logan. She had never expected to see him again. Michael stepped to the podium and called on a teen to open in prayer. Wow, will wonders never cease? Maybe there was more to this big man than met the eye. Michael was apparently the youth leader for this group of teens. Melanie couldn't seem to help herself, her jaw dropped and she stared. Michael caught her eye and smiled.

The scripture that he turned to was a familiar one to Melanie. The story of the prodigal son told in Luke fifteen. He expounded on the unconditional love of the father and the forgiveness that he had for his son. The father was waiting there eagerly to forgive this wayward child. This was a portrait of a father that Melanie couldn't relate to in her own life. Her earthly father wasn't waiting there for her but her heavenly father was. The final comment, that Michael made, really stepped on her toes as she thought about how rotten her father had been to them. Michael said, "And he who is forgiven much loves much. How much do you love others? Do you forgive others the way your father has forgiven you?'

Melanie needed some time to think about these truths and how she had developed an unforgiving attitude concerning her father. It wasn't fun to see yourself as bitter and unforgiving, but if the shoe fits you might as well wear it. She had been unforgiving and bitter. She had also shown prejudice in her attitude toward Michael. That couldn't be what God would want her to do. She had to admit, *Boy, am I a work in progress.*

After the service, she was being greeted by some of the folks in the congregation, when Michael walked over to her and smiled. He just stood in front of her and grinned. He really had the nicest little smile. She realized that it showed off the dimple in his chin. This was a little annoying to Melanie, in a cute kind of way.

"Well if it isn't the cat lady from the other night. Hey Melanie, it's nice to see you again." He stepped in front of her as if daring her not to acknowledge him.

She knew she might as well talk to him since he was standing in her path anyway. "I guess you could tell from my reaction that I was surprised to see you again. Your youth group did a fantastic job with the service this morning. I really enjoyed it." Melanie hoped that she was being friendly without being too familiar. She liked this guy and would like to be on good terms with him since he seemed to be a member of her new church.

Michael glowed in her approval. He obviously was very attached to this group of teens. "I'm just so proud of the kids. They have really worked hard to make today a success."

I understand from Pastor Anthony that you have some experience working in the children's department."

She was really flattered that he checked up on her but how did he know she had been coming to church here? It made her a little nervous. "Yes I have been working in the children's program at my former church in West Virginia for a few years. I enjoy children; they

23

always say exactly what's on their mind." As they were talking she started trying to ease toward the door gradually to make her escape. He started walking beside her and didn't seem to take the hint.

"We really need some help with our youth program. Cindy Bowman, the lady that was working with the girls is having a baby soon so she can't be as involved in their activities." It didn't take a rocket scientist to see where this was heading.

"I really would like to help but I'm just getting my pet shop opened and I just moved here. I have a lot of loose ends to tie up before I'll have very much free time."

"A pet shop, now why should that surprise me? Where is your shop, I might stop by and check it out?"

How could she gracefully get out of this one? "Well it's over on the Beach Road but it's not open for business quite yet. Are you looking for a pet for yourself?"

"No not for me but my niece has been begging for a puppy." The old niece excuse, Melanie had heard that one before.

"Well we should be open soon so keep us in mind." She started walking faster and making her way toward the parking lot. He didn't follow this time.

Whew, that was close. Melanie was going to have to decide if she wanted to dodge this guy or be his friend. Maybe if she explained that she's not interested in dating, he'd agree to a friendship. She would really love to work with those teens. He could have a girlfriend and she was getting ahead of herself. Somehow she got the feeling that he wanted a little more than friendship. She couldn't handle anything like that right now. She sure hoped that he would accept that fact. She wouldn't have to worry about it either way unless he asked her out on a date.

As Melanie was sitting in Old Yeller and thinking about him, he appeared at her window knocking. She almost jumped out of her skin. As she rolled down the window, she got herself under control and smiled at him.

"Hey Michael, did you forget something?"

"I didn't forget exactly but I wondered if you had any plans for lunch? We could go have a bite together and I could tell you more about the youth program" He looked at her hopefully with a cute little boy face. Now she was wondering if a lunch while you were talking about a church program would be considered a date or a meal between friends. She was hungry and she was interested but she didn't want to give this guy the wrong idea. Maybe she'd go and just get this all out in the open with him. She decided to take this opportunity to lay her cards on the table.

"I guess a friendly lunch talking about the kids would be fine. Why don't I follow you to the restaurant?"

He hesitated as if that idea wasn't what he had in mind. "It is a little ways out of town and with gas being so expensive, why don't you just ride with me? I'm parked right over there." He pointed to the same green pickup that she had ridden in when Old Yeller had broken down. It did look a little bit cleaner but she wanted to keep it friendly and nothing remotely like a date.

"I'll tell you what, why not just hop in Old Yeller here and I'll drive?" She could tell that he wasn't thrilled about the idea of riding around in a bright yellow bug but he shrugged his shoulders and walked over to the passenger door and got in. Amazingly, Melanie found herself driving down the road with this man in her car and wondering how in the world she could have let this happen. She must be slipping.

There were several men who would come to the Feed and Seed back home that were interested in dating Melanie and she had no problem turning them down. She had gone on a date here and there but tried to keep any dates that she accepted in a group situation. If she needed an escort for something, she could always get Jerry's friend Bobby. He was a year older than Jerry and a year younger than Melanie. He was what Melanie would consider a safe date. He was from the hills of West Virginia and was so shy it took him months of coming to their house before he would even talk to Melanie without looking at his shoes. She always knew he had a little crush on her but she made sure that he understood she was not interested in a relationship with a man. But that Bobby could be a little thick headed at times.

She'd never forget the day when he tried to kiss her. It took a lot for Melanie not to laugh out loud at his clumsy attempt at romance. They were in the barn working with a baby owl that Bobby had rescued and brought to her for first aide. Melanie had been kneeling down beside the little cage that was sitting on the floor of the barn. He was kneeling beside her. As she got ready to get up, she must have leaned toward him completely by accident. He apparently took this as a sign and puckered his lips out and made this silly smacking noise while moving his face toward hers. She hauled off and decked him right there on the spot. It was a reflex and she doesn't even remember moving. She just popped him right on the jaw as hard as she could. West Virginia girls from the hills were not known as little weaklings and she was mad as a wet hen at the time.

"Bobby, if you ever try that again I'll sick the dog on you, do you understand?" Poor Bobby was so embarrassed that he didn't come back over to their house for a month. She had to sit him down and talk to him and explain that they were just friends and things got smoothed over eventually.

The thought of Michael trying to kiss her didn't make her as mad as it should. Maybe she should go home and practice her right hook on a pillow just to be prepared. Michael Logan is starting to get under her skin. This couldn't be good.

They arrived at the small restaurant and as soon as she parked he got out and came around and opened the car door for her. She could get used to that kind of treatment. He placed his hand in the small of her back as they walked toward the door. This was certainly a new feeling. A feeling of protection which was something she had never felt from a man before, except her brother. The men that she had known in her life so far hadn't been exactly protective. More like the other way around, expecting her to take care of them.

The restaurant was crowded and they had to wait for a table. There was another couple in front of Michael and Melanie who happened to be from their church, although Melanie had not met them, Michael was certainly on friendly terms with them. He struck up a conversation and introduced them to her. She was so embarrassed that she can't remember their names five minutes later. Michael acted like they were there as a couple or something. Now people at church might think they were dating. Melanie was perturbed. They were finally seated at a small table in the corner of the room. Melanie was really feeling nervous by this time and it must have shown because Michael started asking her about the shop. Now when she talked about that shop she could go on and on and before she knew what had happened she was feeling much more at ease. As they talked about Lance, Newman and Pepe', they actually laughed a couple of times and Melanie realized that she was enjoying this a little too much. They needed to get back to business.

"So Michael, you were going to tell me about the youth program." He looked at her a little sideways as if he knew what she was thinking and started telling her about his kids.

"They have come so far this past year. The boys group went on a trip down to the gulf to help out after the hurricanes. This really affected them positively. I think it made them realize how blessed they are. We have had a hurricane or two come through the coast of North Carolina in their lifetime and they have experienced having to be evacuated from their homes. I don't think any of those boys walked away from that trip without thinking that it could have been them."

Melanie was impressed with the unselfish sacrifice of the teens. "Wow, Michael, it sounds like being in this youth group has made a big impact on them. How wonderful you must feel to have the privilege of leading them. God has certainly given you a huge opportunity and along with it responsibility."

Michael looked at her for a moment as if he was surprised at her words. "That is exactly how I feel. I am so grateful that I have the chance to help get these kids going in the right direction toward a life in close fellowship with God, but it humbles me too because something I say or do might have the opposite effect on them. I don't think I've ever had someone understand what a responsibility it can be."

His comment embarrassed her a little because it felt like they had connected somehow. "Well I did work with the children's department back home in West Virginia and I felt that responsibility as I prayed for and worked with those kids. I think if you're going to work with children or teens you have to take it seriously. They are the future of God's church."

Michael leaned toward her and his voice took on an intense serious tone. "Melanie I believe you are the right person to work with the teen girls. The girls didn't get to go to the gulf because they didn't have a female leader that was able to supervise them. These girls are just too interested in clothes and boys and I want to see them more interested in God. Do you think you would reconsider and pray about working with our youth?"

There's nothing like being put on the spot. Melanie did feel a call deep inside her heart that made her think that she was supposed to work with teenagers. She felt she really needed to seek God about this. If she agreed to take on this responsibility, it needed to be because of the kids and not because of Michael.

"I'll pray about it and we'll talk again. That's all I can promise right now."

"That sounds great Melanie because I think God sent you here for this reason. I've been praying for a strong leader for these girls and you just might be the answer to that prayer, maybe along with another prayer or two that I've uttered."

"What does that mean Michael? I want you to understand that I'm not interested in dating anybody right now. I'm not sure what you have in mind but I am just interested in the youth group and not anything personal."

"Did I say anything that made you think I was asking you out? I'm not the kind of guy who would use the youth group to get a date. I really need someone who could help out with these kids right now. Who knows, once you get to know me you could be asking me out?"

She just smiled and shrugged her shoulders. "I wouldn't hold my breath if I were you."

There was no denying that he had her number. There is a lot more to Michael Logan than met the eye.

"Lord what are you getting me in to?"

Chapter Three

It was a beautiful day and Melanie decided to drive her little yellow car to Wilmington to get some supplies for the store. She was alone and it was forecasted to be in the low seventy's that day so she rode with the top down. Oh what a joyful feeling it was for her to drive down that back road and turn on her gospel music and jam with God. She felt so blessed that she could hardly stand it. She had a wonderful time studying her Bible that morning and she felt reassured that God was in control of her life. She was not going to worry about those last minute details for the store. She was trusting God that it would all work out fine.

There was a wooded area on both sides of the road and it reminded Melanie of being home in the woods of West Virginia, without the mountains. Melanie had heard that the locals call that area green swamp. She thought that the woods might have some swamp water in them but she couldn't see it from the road. She was so in awe to be seeing God's creation up close and personal. Looking through a car window just wasn't the same. The air was a little cool but it made her feel so free that she just wanted to raise her hands to heaven. She did raise her arms to the sky for a few seconds but figured she'd better remember that she was supposed to be driving. She could see a couple of rabbits jumping along the side of the road in the brush and she saw a squirrel chattering beside an oak tree. She loved to watch all of God's little creatures.

Then it came to her like a flash. *"I've got it."* She said out loud, *"the name for my shop will be God's Little Creatures. It's perfect and I love it. I'll check on getting the sign made while I'm in Wilmington"*. The name will put the credit for the shop where it was due with God the creator of all those little creatures that she will sell and also all those big creatures that will buy them. He's also the one who should get the credit for a simple country girl from the hills of West Virginia being able to see her dream come true. Realizing this, made Melanie want to raise her hands to heaven again. *"Thank you God"* Melanie made it a few more seconds this time before she had to grab the steering wheel.

It was a good thing she left the boys at home today. Lance would be really annoyed if the breeze was flying through his hair, Newman would be frantic, and Peep' might try to jump out of the car. She was going to have to come up with a system of how to let the boys ride in the car with the top down. She couldn't let them miss out on all the fun. Maybe some type of carriers would be just the thing. She decided that she would have to try out some of the ones out that she would carry in God's Little Creatures.

Thinking about the woods and the animals makes her think of Jerry. How could this have happened to him? How could her baby brother be in prison? At least Momma didn't live to see it. It would have broken her heart. She had been so proud of him. Jerry was such a good upstanding young man before they lost Momma. Then it was like he changed into someone else. Momma had been his rock. If Jesus had been his rock, he would have been able to handle it better.

Jerry and Momma had rarely gone to church. Momma didn't think the good people of the church accepted her. She always thought they talked about her behind her back. Truth be known they most likely did talk about her sometimes because she had occasionally been a little hateful to the town's people but she shouldn't have let that stop her from attending church. Life had hurt her and made her bitter towards others that she considered above her station in life. Jerry had always been very protective of her. From the time he was a little boy and their father had left Momma had called him the man of the house. She always spoiled him and let him get away with more than was good for him but he was basically a good boy.

Melanie had gone to church alone from the time she was twelve. She had gotten invited to a summer camp by the preacher and while she was there, she accepted the Lord as her savior. Her life was never the same after that. She spent the next several years praying for her family and trying to get them to go to church. They had never attended church together until the day of the funeral. Melanie's Momma accepted Christ in the hospital after she was too sick to go, when it was too late. Melanie knew that her mother really regretted the missed opportunities. Jerry was angry at God for her illness. Melanie believes that he is still is angry at God and himself.

After Jerry graduated high School, he went to work at the shirt factory with Momma. They spent a lot of time together. They even started going to the tavern on the weeknights to stop in and have a beer after work. Shortly after this was when he met Rachel.

Rachel was the niece of old Al who ran the local tavern. She was a blonde-haired, blue-eyed pretty little thing. She acted really sweet at first, but Melanie could tell right away that she was spoiled and selfish. Momma had really liked her and encouraged Jerry to ask her out. She liked the fact that Rachel's family was well respected in the community. They started dating and dated for the next four years. Rachel was the type of woman who knew how to get what she wanted from those around her. It wasn't manipulation exactly but she was most definitely used to getting her own way. She had Jerry jumping at her every beck and call. He would have done anything for her and she didn't hesitate to take advantage of him. He was desperately in love with her.

Right about the same time that Jerry was buying a house and planning to get married, Rachel decided she had enough of small town life and without telling Jerry a thing just up and moved to Columbia. To say that Jerry was heartbroken would be an understatement. She met some businessman at the tavern and the next thing anybody knew she had gone. He talked her into moving to Columbia promising a good job and a better life. She was still naive enough to believe him.

This was the same week that they had found out about their Momma's lung cancer. Jerry had to stay in town so that he could be there for his mother during that time. Rachel had been gone about six months before his mother died. The day after the funeral Jerry packed his things and headed for Columbia. He wanted to escape the pain of loosing his Momma and thought he could find a better job, but his primary motivation was to see Rachel again. He just couldn't get over her.

Being left alone was hard for Melanie. The constant reminders in that house broke her heart. Their little family had been held together by their mother. She wasn't perfect but she had given Melanie what she needed more than anything else, which was unconditional love. Loosing that love was like the loss of a piece of who she was. Who else could she depend on? Who else would be there for her? Well she found out it wasn't anybody here on this earth. It was the Lord. This was when she really had to cry out to God to get herself through the pain. He listened and she felt his presence nearer to her in those days than she had ever felt it before.

Melanie quoted one of her favorite scriptures that got her through those days, Jeremiah 3:13 *"I have loved you with an everlasting love; I have drawn you with loving kindness."* The truth had become clear to her, *"He is my true father and he created me just the way I am. I was skillfully wrought it tells me in Psalm 139:15. I am not an accident and I am going to do something with my life."*

This was when Melanie's dream really became clear in her mind of opening her own pet shop. This was when also she decided that she would not depend on another man. She was following her dream because Momma and Jerry hadn't been able to see their dreams become reality. Momma had spent her life taking care of her children and Jerry had loved the wrong woman.

When Jerry got to Columbia, which is a big city in West Virginia, Rachel welcomed him with open arms. She even introduced him to her boss. The businessman that she followed to the city was in the business of drugs. Rachel had become one of his delivery people which they refer to as mules. She also had gotten a habit since she gotten to the big city. The habit was snorting cocaine. Jerry walked right into a nightmare. The better life that Rachel and Jerry had in the city was actually a life of parties, drugs and organized crime.

During this time Jerry called Melanie faithfully every Sunday. He told her about his wonderful job and his new apartment. He told her that he and Rachel were finally going to get married. He made it sound like he was getting everything that he had always wanted, but she sensed something wasn't quite right. She couldn't put her finger on it but his words of happiness and his dull flat voice didn't match. She was so wrapped up in her own pain and grief that she didn't do anything. She would always regret not doing anything. She was so busy working and going to School and taking care of herself. When she looked back on that time, she believed that she had been selfishly focused on her own life and neglected her brother when he needed her most. She had let him down. He never felt that way but Melanie did.

Melanie found out the truth about four months later when Jerry called her from jail. He loved that girl so much that he couldn't deny her anything. She needed more and more money to support her drug habit. He couldn't give her enough by just being a delivery boy. Rachel had arranged for the boss to let him handle a big drug deal. They were getting a shipment in from Mexico and all he had to do was pick the drugs up and make the payment. The big deal turned out to be a sting operation by undercover police. Melanie's brother ended up in jail. The amount of drugs was so large that he knew he was facing some serious time in prison. His primary thought had still been for Rachel. He didn't want her arrested or involved with the police. He made a plea bargain deal. He pled guilty to drug trafficking charges to keep Rachel from being arrested. His deal unfortunately didn't do anything to stop the publicity. He made his own choices and he accepted the responsibility for them. What the law and the press don't know was that Rachel had been behind that drug deal. Jerry had taken his punishment like the man that his Momma always wanted him to be and he protected his woman by taking all the blame.

Melanie found a little bit of comfort in knowing this. Even after all the things he did, she still believed her brother had a good heart.

He was just a humble country boy who got involved with the wrong woman. But he loved her then and he loves her still.

Back home in West Virginia it was the talk of the town. Old Al at the tavern blamed Jerry for getting Rachel involved with those wicked people. He didn't hesitate to tell anyone that would listen how Melanie's brother turned out to be a drug dealer. He gave detailed embellished accounts about how Jerry had led poor innocent Rachel down the path of destruction and now she was hooked on drugs and it was entirely his fault. He let the whole town know that Jerry had turned out to be no good just like his father or so the story went.

People started avoiding walking down the same side of the street with Melanie. Customers at the Feed and Seed would refuse to let her wait on them. She was guilty by association. It was a dark time in her life. She had been raised in that town and it had been her home. Even today the only family that she had left, except Jerry, was in that town. Her mother's sister Rose was still living there along with a few cousins. Melanie had become a woman of solitude in those last months. She just lived for the day when she would be able to get away from there. The Lord was what had kept her going. The dream gave her a reason to go on.

Melanie wrote her brother Jerry a letter every Sunday. Sometimes he wrote back sometimes he didn't. She loved her brother even though he'd made some mistakes. She wanted to show him the unconditional love that she knew their Momma would have. Her deepest prayer was that he would become a Christian in prison. She knew it must be a hard life being in prison but the one thing that made Melanie feel better about the situation was the fact that they have an excellent prison ministry. She knew her brother would be given the opportunity to hear about God's love. Her prayer is that he will take that opportunity.

But this was a new day and Melanie would try to forget those things behind her and press forward towards her new life, her new life and her wonderful new shop. She's gotten every detail planned down to the brands of pet food that she planed to carry and who she will purchase it from. She had just a few more details to finalize and she'll be ready for her grand opening.

Today she was taking care of some of those details. But the first thing she'd better do is stop someplace and buy a map of Wilmington because she believed that she might just be a little lost. She had several places that she needed to find today. Her final stop will be a shipping office where she would be picking up two very important pieces of cargo. One was an African Spider Monkey and the other a Boa Constrictor. Melanie only hoped that they had enough common sense to keep the two shipments separated. She already had a buyer for the snake.

A strange and very tattooed man had come into the shop a couple of weeks ago. He told Melanie that his name was Harry and he heard about a new pet shop so he decided to check it out. Melanie was a little nervous when she saw him but as he began to talk and tears formed in his eyes, she knew that she was just the person to help him. It seemed that he and his wife were getting a divorce and the wife had gotten custody of their snake. The man wanted to get another Boa right away to let his wife know that he was not going to sit around and brood about it. He wanted to show her that he was moving on with his life. Melanie thought that he had a healthy attitude and the profit that she planed to make on the transaction came at just the right time. A little extra cash would come in handy to get everything needed for the shop.

The African Spider Monkey was really for Melanie. He was very expensive, but she had always wanted one. He'll have to be sold eventually she knew, but she wanted some time to enjoy him first. Some people may think that this breed of monkeys wouldn't make a good pet. Melanie was hoping that this one would be trainable since he was still young.

She planed to enjoy all her animals. The monkey will help draw the townspeople into the shop. Getting the word out in the area that "Gods little Creatures" was not just another kitten and puppy store would help Melanie to get a customer base established. Exotic animals were hard to find but she had a few sources. The niche that she is making for herself is how she planed to bring in enough revenue to keep the shop solvent. She's not expecting to make a living just by selling dog food.

Her errands were completed and as she pulled into the parking lot to the shipping office, she was so excited that she couldn't stand it. There seemed to be a slight problem developing when Melanie walked in the front door. People were scurrying around all over the place shouting and standing on the furniture. It seemed that they have had a bit of a problem that was about to become her problem. The spider monkey, that Melanie later named Felix, had an undiscovered talent. He knew how to unlock the clasps on animal cages. Both the monkey and the Boa were loose in the shipping office.

When Melanie heard that they had lost the snake she chuckled because how could you loose a twenty foot snake. She kept a cool head because those people were acting nuts and she calmly asked if anybody had an egg. Of course they all looked at her like she had grown another head. She calmly explained that this snake has a particular liking for chicken eggs and it was always easier to catch anything with a little bait. She was quickly accommodated with a couple of boiled eggs from somebody's lunch. Melanie set up a little trap for the Boa and had him safely back in custody in twenty minutes. Now Felix was a little easier, all Melanie had to do was hold a banana out in his direction and he jumped onto her shoulder. They were fast friends and she quickly forgave him for this little adventure. She could certainly understand how he could have gotten bored cooped up in that cage and was most likely just looking for a little companionship. Melanie learned a long time ago that food was always a good way to get an animal to trust you. Well in the Boa's case his trust was misplaced because he got caught, but it was for his own good. Harry the tattoo guy will give this Boa a good home.

Melanie decided that it might be a good idea to put the top up on the car for the ride home. She figured that the snake and the monkey had probably had enough excitement for one day. Felix was good company on the ride home. He kept up a steady chatter and Melanie talked to him as well. They had a good conversation although they didn't understand one another. Melanie knew that an animal feels more secure if they are accustomed to their owner's voice. Once you gain an animal's trust you can usually teach them to respond to some simple requests. Felix had to stay in the carrier in the car but already Melanie could see that he was going to learn quickly. This was what she was meant to do, work with animals. It felt so good to know that you are doing what you were meant to do.

When they got home, Melanie had to introduce Felix to the boys. Now it's highly unlikely that Lance or Newman had ever seen a monkey before. This could get interesting. Pepe' who you might say was not a real bright thinker should adjust pretty quickly. As Melanie brought the snake cage into the spare bedroom the boys didn't have mush of a reaction. They were used to having extra animals around and they had seen a few snakes. It seemed best to be sure that the cage was padlocked though because Pepe' would make a meal for the large snake.

Melanie decided that Felix would stay in the main house with the family. She wanted to spend some time training him before she opened the shop. She fit him with a collar and a leash so that she could control his movements while she had him out of the cage. So Melanie slowly sat Felix's cage on the floor to see what the cats would do. Newman, who is curious as they say cats are, stuck his nose through the bars on the cage. When Felix started chattering hello, Newman did a back flip he jumped back so fast. Lance just started walking in that direction sort of slowly and stopped about a foot away from the front of the cage and looked in that direction. When he got a glance of that monkey he actually took off running in the direction of the bedroom. He very seldom moved that fast. Pepe' the dog was just excited in general and barked at the monkey in the cage a couple times and then came over to Melanie and started jumping up and down to get her attention. He seemed to think she should notice how brave he was and reward him. So she rubbed his little head and put him outside in the backyard to do his business. They were all just going to have to get along. It might be a long night.

Chapter Four

It was her big day and Melanie was so excited that she wanted to jump up and down. She had been up since before dawn dancing around the house with her praise music on. She was so thankful to God for this blessing. She thought to herself, *I am actually going to be a business owner and God's Little Creatures is opening its doors.* She hoped she had thought of everything that could arise but only time would tell.

The shop was located in a strip mall with a glass store front window. Melanie had dressed the windows to attract attention from anyone who happened to be passing by. She wanted people to feel free to come in and browse. The interior of the store was broken into three sections. The first section was the shelving area at the front of the store which was just beyond the check out counter. The shelves held a large variety of pet food and supplies. There was also a shelf devoted entirely to pet toys. Melanie believed in keeping pets stimulated. There was also a section of aquariums and fish related items. She had decided to carry some unusual and exotic fish and snakes which were housed in the aquarium area as well. Melanie had a theory that people who live at the coast will be very interested in a variety of fish. She had also made contact with new suppliers that have the contacts to order any hard to find species. The back section of the shop was the live animal section. This area was divided up by cages and various habitats for the animals that were in stock for sale to the public. There was a puppy pen with a play and sleep area.

There was also a cat and kitten pen similar in nature to the puppy pen. The there was a habitat for various birds and other cages for the rest of the animals. Melanie had a special cage se up for Felix the monkey with a tree habitat. He would be in the center of the live animal section.

There was a jungle mural on the side wall and a forest mural on the back wall where the cages were. This was Melanie's dream shop and it had a personality of its own. All the animals were in place and all the shelves were stocked. Her pockets were empty but her heart was full. Today was the grand opening. She had even brought the boys to the shop today to share in this moment.

Melanie had advertised in the local paper and put out flyers announcing the grand opening. The local radio station had promised to do a live interview around noon. She was serving animal theme refreshments. They included a fruit arrangement with a porcupine made from a pineapple, and a vegetable arrangement with broccoli in the shape of a furry little puppy, and the original creation of a cake in the shape of a Siamese cat. Melanie was wondering if any people would come to eat all of this food. She was inviting folks to bring their pets in with them so she had dog and cat treats for the visiting animal friends. She felt so nervous that she thought she might throw up.

The doors opened at exactly nine o'clock and Melanie didn't see a single person until nine thirty. That was when she spotted one single strange looking person. It was a teenaged girl with several piercings, very dark hair and a very white face. She had her fingernails painted black and her lips colored a dark color that made her look kind of spooky. Melanie thought about it and decided that after her experience with the snake guy, she shouldn't judge a book by its cover. This was a little hard for her because she has never seen people like this in the hills of West Virginia.

"Hello, may I help you with something?" When the girl looked at Melanie and she saw pain reflected in her eyes. Melanie immediately recognized the pain because it was something she had a lot of experience with. The girl looked her straight in the eye and surprised her by saying,

"My name is Autumn and I've always loved animals. I have experience working with the public and running a cash register. I am a hard worker and wouldn't be afraid to clean up any messes the animals make. I had two dogs and a hamster when I was little. I am staying in town with my Aunt right now because my mother couldn't take care of me. I am seventeen and I would do just about anything if you would give me a job in your shop."

Melanie was a little taken back by the girl's bold proclamation but also a little impressed. She realized how much courage and spunk it took for the girl to approach her like that. She was a strange looking child but there was something about her that Melanie couldn't resist. She felt a pull from God so strong to help this girl that she did something totally crazy. Without having one single customer or taking in one single dollar, she hired Autumn as a part-time employee to work at God's Little Creatures. After all Autumn was God's creation and that was Melanie's dream, to help take care of God's Creatures. She just didn't know they were going to include the human variety.

Opening day did improve and customers starting trickling in. They sold a few fish, an aquarium, a parakeet, and a guinea pig along with the necessary equipment. Harry, the snake guy came by and picked up the Boa. This caused quite a stir among the other customers. Melanie got a big fat check from him and she felt like she was actually in business. All in all it was a pretty good opening day. There was a lot of food left over but she fed some of the fruits and veggies to the animals. The left over cat cake went home with Melanie and the boys. The boys don't get any of it but she thought Helen might enjoy a piece or two over coffee. It would be a good excuse to visit. She just couldn't wait to share the news of how opening day went.

Autumn had turned out to be a hard worker. She had a desire to be accepted that came through loud and clear. It turned out interestingly enough, that she knew some kids that were in the youth program at Melanie's new church. She seemed interested in hearing more about it. Her Aunt according to Autumn, might be having a hard time with understanding her and her desire to dress and look differently. Melanie would be the first to admit she wondered about Autumn at first because of her looks, but after she took the time to get to know the girl, she found herself liking her despite her odd appearance. She also had shown a keen wit that belied her age. It took a little while for her to relax around Melanie but by mid-afternoon she surprised her once again.

An elderly lady came in to look at birds and Autumn was helping her. The lady looked at Autumn and with a loud and rude voice said, "What's wrong with you girl, are trying to be a pin cushion or something?" Autumn came back without missing a beat, No Mam, I'm studying to be a nurse and I have to practice sticking needles in myself. It's a good thing I get this practice because I might have to stick a needle in you someday."

The lady looked at her and thought about it and started chuckling, "go on with you now girlie, you're pulling my leg." Autumn just smiled and brought the ladies purchases to the register. Melanie was smiling too, as she turned to finish stocking the shelves that she had been working on. Melanie decided that she was really going to like that girl

Melanie had another surprise about mid-morning when a delivery person brought a bouquet of big yellow sunflowers. They were so beautiful and just exactly what she would have picked for herself. She couldn't imagine who could have sent them. Maybe Jerry had found a way to somehow send them from prison. When she read the card her jaw dropped. They were from Michael Logan congratulating her on opening day. It was really a surprise that went well beyond friendship.

Sunflowers were Melanie's favorite type of flower. Not carnations or roses or even daisies but sunflowers. She always thought that they had personality. The inner circle seemed to smile and radiate petals of happiness all around it. She thought that it would be nice to have that kind of effect on people. The fact that after a few short conversations, Michael Logan knew enough about Melanie to send sunflowers to her was kind of eerie.

She found out from church friends that Michael was a construction worker. Well technically, a General Contractor but still a construction worker. She also suspected that he liked NASCAR Racing because she recognized a license plate on his pickup truck that was associated with a NASCAR driver. It's not that Melanie didn't like NASCAR because she used to watch racing with her brother on Sundays. It's just that if she wanted to pick two things that would not be on her list of desirable traits for a man they would be the fact that he was a macho construction worker and liked racing. It was hard for Melanie to picture this person as the sensitive type. These things just don't add up in her brain with the guy who goes to her church and works with the youth. It didn't seem like he would be the type to send sunflowers either. She thought she might need to investigate him further just for her own piece of mind.

That was exactly what she decided she would do the following day. Michael had mentioned that he had been working on some condos on the ocean front and Melanie decided to cruise up Ocean Drive and take a look just to see if she could spot his truck in the neighborhood. She loved the beach even in the winter. Just looking at the water made her think about how awesome God is and how wonderful his creation is.

It wasn't hard at all to find that familiar green truck parked in an abandoned parking lot close to some condos undergoing renovations. Melanie's immediate problem was how to approach Michael without being too obvious. Well a nice walk on the beach might be in order. She parked Old Yeller a couple of blocks down from the place that she saw his truck and she got out and started to walk down the beach in his direction. She told herself that she wasn't chasing after him but just giving them an opportunity to meet again, accidentally on purpose. Maybe if she could see him in the raw element of his construction job she might be able to fit him into a compartment that she had neatly filed away in her brain. As long as he's filed in a compartment he wouldn't surprise her again like he did yesterday with those sunflowers. She had no clue how to handle surprises like that. She liked them but they threw her off balance.

She walked up the beach and when she got to the construction site, she just stopped and watched a little while. She spotted Michael right away recognizing his broad shoulders. She could tell he was a person in authority even though he wasn't loud or bossy in any way. The way the men acted was friendly but respectful. He was definitely a leader but didn't take advantage of his position. He led by example while he worked right along bedside his men. A couple of the men saw her and started pointing her way and talking so she thought she had better make her presence known.

Melanie boldly walked up to the group of men and asked if Michael Logan was there. "Hey Boss Man, there's a lady here to see you." He looked over and a surprised look registered on his face followed by a smile. This caused quite a stir and a little ribbing as Michael came over and led Melanie to a more private area off to one side of the building site.

Melanie felt a little embarrassed and her mouth got dry and suddenly she didn't know what to say. "Hey Michael, I wanted to thank you for the flowers."

He looked at her like he just couldn't believe she was there and said, "If that was all it took for you to show up, I'll send you flowers every day."

Melanie knew it would seem false to act like she hadn't looked him up. "I just wanted to see you in your working environment. A construction worker who sent me sunflowers, I can't figure you out."

He chuckled and shook his head, "Now that should be my line. You are a puzzle to me Melanie Byron. You certainly keep a guy on his toes. How about we walk over to the coffee shop and talk about it some more, we have an audience."

She looked back and every man on that site had stopped what they were doing and were watching them intently. "Sounds like a plan to me." She looked back at his men and smiled and gave a little wave and took Michael's hand as they walked away. "I'll wink at them and give them something to talk about."

Now if you really want to get them talking I could kiss you right here in plain sight." He looked at her with that little boy grin that was starting to make her toes curl.

"I hardly think that would be necessary."

He broke in to a laugh and put his arm around her, resting on her back. "May not be necessary but it could be nice. You might want to think about that."

Melanie certainly would never admit to him that she had already thought about it, against her better judgment. Her face turned a little red but she didn't want him to know why. "How about that cup of coffee you suggested?"

Sounds like a plan." He threw her words back at her. She wondered to herself, *why do I seem to act like an idiot when I get around this guy? It is really beginning to get on my nerves.* Melanie decided to concentrate on the sound of the ocean behind them and not the fact that he still had his arm around her in a very possessive way. She couldn't believe she let herself get into this situation. *What was I thinking? I'm getting in over my head here and can't seem to stop. Momma always told me I should never trust or depend on a man. I really wish I could believe this one would be dependable because it sure would be nice to have someone solid to depend on.*

They arrived at the coffee shop and found a small table in the corner. They gave the waitress their order and Melanie was still wondering what she was doing there. Michael was looking as pleased as punch with himself and that kind of annoyed her and flattered her at the same time.

"So you liked the flowers, huh?"

I really love sunflowers and they were just the thing to make my grand opening day more special." She started talking about opening day and the snake man and Felix the monkey and, to her surprise; he seemed really interested in hearing about it. Sometimes when Melanie was excited she tended to talk a little too much. Before she realized what she was saying she mentioned something about making her dream come true for Momma and Jerry. He frowned and stopped her in mid sentence.

Just hold up there a minute Melanie, just who is Jerry? Did you have a boyfriend before you moved here?"

She realized what she had said and could have kicked herself. She should have remembered she had never been very good at keeping secrets. I didn't have a boyfriend back home, Jerry is my baby brother. He's in prison back in West Virginia." She was really annoyed at herself, so much for overcoming the stigma of a felon for a brother. She sat there paralyzed with fear wondering what his reaction might be.

"I'd like for you to tell me about your brother sometime when you feel ready." That was all he said and then he reached over and took her hand across the table and said, "Now tell me more about your first day."

"I really did want to talk to you about Autumn. She is a seventeen year old girl that I hired to work in the shop. She acts and dresses a little different but I felt her need for acceptance deep inside me and I really think she needs help."

"Melanie, is this girl going to be someone who might take advantage of you?"

She had to smile at this because the idea was so sweet and caring but kind of dumb at the same time. "I have enough common sense not to let a kid take advantage of me no matter how needy she is. I just thought maybe you could come by and meet her and talk to her about youth group."

"Are you inviting me over to see you at the shop?"

"Yes, I guess I am. Not to see me exactly but to meet Autumn. She is going to work in the afternoons from four to six and on Saturday mornings."

"So you don't want to see me again?"

"Of course I'll see you again we go to the same church."

"Melanie, you know what I'm asking. When we first met you told me that you weren't interested in dating. Have you changed your mind about that?"

"How about we just consider ourselves friends and see how that works out before we call ourselves dating?"

I want to be more than your friend Melanie; I want to be perfectly honest with you about that."

"Michael, I'm not sure I'm ready for anything else. I have a really hard time trusting people and I don't know if I can handle a man-woman relationship. I have never really seriously dated a man before."

"Well maybe it's time you gave it a try. The way you learn to trust is by getting to know another person. Dating is the way people get to know each other better. It's as simple as that."

"Why don't we try a few friendly get-togethers first? I want you to understand they will not be dates. I don't want to date anybody right now"

Michael made it sound so reasonable but I'm not ready to concede just yet. Boy she thought to herself, am gullible or what?

"Alright Melanie, would you like to get together Saturday night and see a movie?"

She only hesitated a few moments but the silence was tense.

"As long as it's a G or PG rated movie, I will accept your invitation to get together." By this time she was feeling a little silly and couldn't help but smile. He smiled back and we got up to leave.

"Where is your car parked, I'll walk you back." Now she sure would hate for him to see how she'd checked him out from two blocks away but what could she do?

"It's a couple of blocks down the beach." He just took her hand and started down the street. He might be a little bit of a gentleman since he didn't remark on the location of her car. Then he let her hand go and did that thing with his hand on the small of her back. Who was she kidding this guy is a gentlemen all the way. Boy was she in trouble. She breathed a prayer. *"Lord, please show me how, to do the right thing. I really need help with this situation. Is it part of your plan for Michael and I to be more than friends? Please show me the right way. Amen.*

Chapter Five

Melanie got a call on Friday at the shop from Pastor Anthony. It seemed that the regular Sunday School teacher for the five to seven year old class had a family emergency. The assistant was out of town and they needed someone to fill in on Sunday. She made the arrangements to get the teaching materials and lesson plan and before she knew what was happening, she was a Sunday School teacher again. *That is so much like God,* Melanie thought. *He gives me the desires of my heart sometimes even when I don't always realize what they are. I have really missed my Sunday School kids from the church back home.*

She had to give up her class several months ago when some of the ladies started making noises about a drug dealer's sister teaching their children. It was one of the things that hurt her the most. She loved those kids and they had loved her. She had put a lot of time and energy into that class and she was so hurt when she was asked to step down for the good of the entire congregation.

Melanie looked at herself in the mirror and started talking to her image. *This is going to be an eventful weekend, my first friendly get together (not a date) with Michael and I'm going to be teaching again. I think some strategic planning is in order. First what should I wear and how will I handle this evening? I have spent a lot of time this week wondering how I got myself into this. Michael is not part of my life's plan. He is just sort of sneaking up on me. I'm not sure why he even likes me. My long curly brown hair is kind of wild and not cut in one of the current styles. I don't have expensive clothes that flatter my figure. I have never really wanted to attract attention to myself. I just wear whatever I can find on sale that I like. Jeans and casual tops are my normal clothes. I'm not really sure what to wear tonight. I'm thinking about wearing a little makeup. My eyes are just plain brown not exotic blue or green. I don't usually wear any makeup because I have long eyelashes and my eyes are a little larger than average. I think that my eyes are my best feature. My Momma used to tell me that I had a heart shaped face. She said that it showed the world what a big heart I have. She used to say she was making the best of what the good Lord gave her when she was dressing up to go out. I guess I should try making the best of what the good Lord gave me tonight and see what happens. A little shopping might be in order.*

Melanie waited until Autumn came in and she took the rest of the afternoon off to get ready. She found a really nice dress in a little shop just down the street from the pet shop. The dress was clingy and elegant without being too dressy. It was subtle print in browns and greens and it was cut nicely so that her frame gave the illusion of being taller and her legs looked longer.

She felt really pretty in the dress and Mrs. Williams at the dress shop told her the most important thing about buying a new dress is that it makes you feel pretty. Melanie really hoped Michael liked it because even on sale it was much more than she usually would spend on herself.

Michael was coming over to Melanie's house to pick her up. The boys will have a chance to check him out. He'd met Lance but Newman and Pepe' were going to be a surprise. Lance was really the best judge of character. When her car had broken down and Michael rescued them, Lance was too emotional to be able to really make a wise judgment. Tonight if Lance was in any way friendly to Michael when he came to pick Melanie up, she will feel reassured.

The time had flown by and Melanie was running a little late as usual. She just couldn't decide how she should wear her hair. She usually wore it pulled back because there's just so much of it.

Tonight she thought it might be a nice change to wear it down. The only problem being that it was hard to tame into some kind of reasonable style. *Oh well she tells herself, this is as good as it gets.*

When the doorbell rang she was hopping on one foot looking around the house for her lost shoe. Pepe' had been at it again. Having the urge to chew her shoes was one of the things she was trying to break him from. She hadn't found all his hiding places in the new house yet, so she found herself answering the door with one shoe on and one shoe off. This made her appear a little crooked but as she pulled the door open, Michael didn't seem to mind.

"Hey Michael, I'm not quite ready won't you come in." She opened the screened door and he came into the house. He was silent was for a couple of minutes and she wondered what was wrong with him.

Michael was struck dumb by her beauty. This woman was amazing. She looked like she should be in the movies or something. He knew that she was pretty, but wow.

"Wow, Melanie you are beautiful. I mean I knew you were beautiful but you are really gorgeous."

Melanie didn't know what to say because she was certainly not used to compliments. Her face turned red but she was secretly pleased. "Thanks Michael, you look very nice too." He did look very handsome in his khaki pants and his blue polo shirt.

"Can I help you with your shoe?" He asked her this with the typical grin that he seems to have on his face when he was around her.

"No thanks why don't you have a seat and I'll be out shortly." Melanie went upstairs to the bedroom and closed the door. She had no idea if the missing shoe was in the bedroom so she figured she had better just find another pair. She finally found some pumps in the box labeled shoes in the back of the closet and checked her appearance in the mirror again. She peeped out into the living room and Lancelot was lying on the couch beside Michael as he rubbed his back. It would seem that Michael had certainly passed the Lancelot test.

They had dinner at a really nice seafood restaurant that was on the ocean. The view was beautiful as the colored spotlights of the restaurant shined out across the water. It gave Melanie a peaceful feeling just watching the water and not talking. It was such a wonder to her that they could be silent, yet together. She felt in tune with Michael knowing he was appreciating the scenery with her.

"When I consider the heavens, the work of thy fingers, the moon and the stars that thou hast ordained; what is man that thou art mindful of him; and the son of man that thou visitest him?"

She spoke before she realized it. God just seemed so near as they gazed out across the ocean. Michael turned his head and looked at her tenderly. "You are truly a rare woman Melanie. Not too many women would sit in a romantic restaurant with a man and be thinking about God." He took her hand in his across the table and just sort of held it gently. "I can't stop looking at you tonight. You are so lovely and it shines through on your face from the inside where your sweetness is." He continued to hold her hand and the whole situation was a little bit overwhelming for her.

"Thank you for the kind words, but please don't think that I'm more than I am Michael. I'm a simple woman from West Virginia who has made some mistakes and will probably make some more. I was practically shunned in my home town when everything happened with my brother. People didn't want me teaching their children in church anymore. I'm no prize, believe me."

"Melanie, don't you know that you are a prize to God. He created you just the way that you are for his purpose. I think he did a really nice job. You would be a prize to me too Melanie if you were mine."

Okay this was getting a little to intense for Melanie. This man had struck her speechless. She never had a lack of something to say in almost any situation.

How about a little help here Lord? Psalm 91:15 came to her mind, *He shall call upon me and I will answer him; I will be with him in trouble.*

The waiter came and asked them if they were ready to order. Melanie was very happy to see him. *Thanks Lord.* They ordered the food and the rest of the dinner was nice. He told her about his family and his job. She told him about the kids that she taught back home and how she would be filling in at church this Sunday.

Michael had a large family. There were two brothers who were older and one sister who was a year younger. They were all married. The sister was the only sibling that lived nearby but they all got together pretty regularly for holidays and special occasions. His mother lived about a block from him and he kept a pretty close eye on her. His father had passed away two years ago from a heart attack. His mother was still having a hard time learning to live on her own.

Melanie remembered hearing that if a man is good to his mother, he will be good to his wife. This might be an old wife's tale but it seemed logical to her. It sounded to Melanie as if Michael is very good to his mother.

"Michael, you're a really nice guy and your good looking and hard working. Why haven't you gotten married and started a family of your own?" He seems like such a good catch to Melanie. It's a wonder somebody hadn't snatched him up yet.

"I have been waiting for God to send the right woman." He seemed to search for the right words. "I have dated a couple of women that I met through church functions but I never felt like any of them were the one that God had for me. I don't want to settle for somebody just to get married, I want the one special one that will be my helpmate. Does that make sense to you?"

"Yes, it makes perfect sense to me. I haven't prayed for a mate because I planned never to marry but I can certainly understand how you feel." Melanie hoped he wouldn't ask her why she planned not to marry because she really didn't want to get into it to with him. It was so deep and personal and she didn't think she could explain it at all.

"Michael, what movie were we going to see?" She glanced at her watch and saw that they had been talking for a while and the time had gone by quickly.

"Well, we have two choices of movies that we might want to see. Either the new comedy cartoon movie or the new romantic comedy." He showed no sign indicating which one he would prefer. This could be a good way to see how macho he was.

"I think that I'd like to see the romantic comedy." Melanie was testing him a little bit. She knew that sitting through a chick flick would be torture for her brother. She wondered how Michael would feel about it.

Surprisingly, he didn't seem to mind. "Sounds good, we'd better get going." He picked up his credit card receipt and came around the table as she started getting up. Then he did the arm behind her back thing again. She told herself, *I've really got to get used to being around a guy with good manners, so it doesn't surprise me so much.*

The movie was funny and sweet and they had a lot of fun together. They laughed and Melanie cried a little too at the sad part. It started getting a little too serious, so she threw some popcorn at him to lighten things up. Michael seemed to have a great sense of humor. He really needed one if he planned to hang around with Melanie. She didn't believe that God meant for his people to walk around with long faces all the time. Her philosophy was that the joy of the Lord was one of God's gifts. People could find peace and joy even in midst of their problems. At least they could try. It had not always been easy.

Before Melanie knew it, Michael was pulling up into her driveway to bring her home. She didn't know what to expect when he walked her to the door, but he was a perfect gentlemen. He escorted her to the door and waited while she unlocked it and turned the light on. Then he just smiled and lightly touched her arm lightly as he said, ". I can't tell you how much I enjoyed tonight, I had a wonderful time. Can we get together again soon?"

"I'll see you at church Sunday morning. I'm looking forward to teaching Sunday School, and don't forget to stop by the store so that I can introduce you to Autumn. I'm praying that she'll start coming to church with me and get involved in your youth group."

"How about coming over to eat lunch at my mother's house after church? I'd really like for you to meet her."

"I don't know Michael; I don't want to give people the wrong idea."

"What do you mean the wrong idea? Is there something wrong with you meeting my mother?" he sounded a little peeved at the idea.

"People would talk about us Michael, a man doesn't bring a woman to meet his mother unless they are serious."

"I am serious Melanie." He looked at her with those green eyes of his and she lost her ability to speak again. She just looked at him, cutting her eyes sideways to let him know that she didn't want to talk about it. The words that came out of her mouth were not the ones she planned to say. She found herself saying, "I'd really enjoy having lunch with you and your mother."

She could tell that he was trying not to be smug. "There might be a couple of other people there from my family but it will be really casual." He said this quickly like he hoped she wouldn't really pay attention but she heard it loud and clear. This would be a family dinner.

Melanie was really upset with herself. *What am I thinking? Here I go again getting myself into something I might regret later.*

"Sounds good, I'll see you on Sunday." Then she opened the door and went in and said, "Goodnight," as he stood there on the porch looking kind of silly with that grin of his. "Goodnight Melanie."

Melanie really wanted to sit and think about the things that they both had said and done tonight but she didn't have time. She had a Sunday School lesson to get planned and because the shop was open tomorrow; she wouldn't have as much time to prepare as she would like.

Sunday morning dawned and Melanie had worked late on Friday night and part of Saturday evening preparing the lesson for the children. She had planned a little activity to get them interested in their lesson. Since the lesson was on Noah and the animals, she got a little carried away when she decided to make some cardboard cutouts of animals and let each child pretend to be an animal on the ark. She thought they could start a little conversation back and forth with the children being the animals and her being Noah.

Twelve children showed up for the five to seven year old class. The room was a little small for the children to pretend to be animals and move around so they went outside for their lesson, after they prayed and took up the money. The back and forth conversation between the animals and Noah was a big hit. Each child had to say something about their experience on the ark in the character of their animal. There were two children that especially touched Melanie's heart.

A little boy named Joshua who was blond and blue eyed and had glasses. He wanted to talk about bugs. He started asking questions about the insects on the ark. Now to tell you the truth Melanie had never thought about insects on the ark, but after considering it, there had to be some or they wouldn't have survived the flood. So they turned over the porcupine and made him a spider so that Joshua could represent the insects on the ark. When Joshua found out that Melanie had a pet shop, he immediately started looking at her like she walked on water or something. The little guy was just so cute and so smart Melanie just wanted to pinch him.

The other child that really melted her heart was Laura. She wanted to be the puppy on the ark. The puppy told everybody that she wanted the flood to be over so that she could go home with a nice little girl and be loved. It was pretty obvious that this child wanted a puppy in the worst kind of way that only a child can want something. After class she stayed behind as the other children went to service just to ask about what kind of puppies were in the pet shop. The longing in her eyes was something you couldn't miss. Melanie wondered who her parents were and if they would be interested in buying a puppy for her.

As Melanie made her way to the sanctuary, she spotted Michael talking to some friends over to one side. She didn't really acknowledge him in any way; she just found a good place to sit about the middle of the church. She liked to sit in a different area each service so that she wouldn't get too used to sitting in the same place every Sunday. She thought that it made things more interesting if you move around and sat near different people. She had managed to meet more of the church members this way. She was reading her church bulletin and not really paying attention when she felt a large presence sit down beside her. She looked up and there was Michael looking over at her. Melanie had never had a boyfriend or male family member for that matter who sat with her at church. She didn't like the fact that everybody would know they were friends and probably think he is her boyfriend. Gossip can be so hurtful sometimes.

"Michael, don't you usually sit with your family?" She didn't want to be rude but she wouldn't mind if he sat someplace else.

"I'd rather sit with you and since you're going to lunch with me at my mother's, we won't have to find each other after the service since we're already sitting together."

Why does he have these logical explanations for everything that make her feel petty for objecting? "I guess that makes sense but everyone in church are going to think we're an item." He grinned over at her and looked smug. "We are an item; you just haven't figured it out yet."

Melanie gave him a dirty look and moved over so we wouldn't be sitting so close to each other. "We are not an item Michael Logan," she harshly spoke in a whispering voice.

Melanie wasn't as quiet as she thought she was, because the lady behind them was chuckling behind her hand.

This just infuriated her more and it took her a whole song to decide to not let Michael Logan ruin her Sunday worship. She thought, *I'll just ignore him for the rest of the service.*

He wasn't as easy to ignore as she thought he would be. When they began to sing, his voice was a rich baritone, and even though he was a little off key, it held such sincerity as he sang about the grace of God that she couldn't help but look over at him. When he saw her looking he winked at her. She turned her head and focused on the music and why she was here. Psalm 92:13 says; *"Those that be planted in the house of the Lord shall flourish in the courts of our God."* She made a decision as the thoughts ran through her head. *I'm staying planted in this church and nobody will make me leave except God.*

Chapter Six

After church, Michael and Melanie were stopped by several people who wanted to say hello. He introduced her to some folks she hadn't had the opportunity to meet yet. There were usually around three hundred people attending for Sunday morning service so there were a lot of them she didn't know. One nice looking young couple came over and Michael introduced them as his sister Krystal and her husband David. Melanie noticed that a little girl was standing beside them.

It was Laura, the little girl from Sunday School, who wanted a puppy. She knelt down and shook her hand. "Hello Laura, it's nice to see you again." The girl barely looked her way as she ran up to Michael and grabbed his legs hugging him and saying, "Hey Uncle Mike, are you coming to Granny's for Sunday lunch today?" *He's nice to animals and kids. Is this guy for real?*

Uncle Mike picked her up and gave her a big hug. "Sure am Little Bit and Melanie is coming with me." He looked over at her and grinned.

"I didn't know Michael was your Uncle Mike. Do you mind if I come over to your Granny's with him?"

The little girl reached over and gave her a hug and said, "Okay, are you bringing any puppies from your store?" Her parents groaned and Michael looked amused. "She found out about the shop already?"

"We talked about animals in Sunday School and Laura shared her desire for a puppy with the class." Melanie looked over at the child and gave her an encouraging smile.

"She let us be the animals in the ark and I was the puppy." The little girl looked eagerly at her mother for approval.

"It sounds like you liked having Melanie as your teacher this morning." Krystal looked warmly at the child giving her undivided attention.

"She was nice and I had fun but I still love Miss Emily too."

"Of course you do. Are you ready to go to your Granny's?"

"We'll see you guys at Mom's" Michael grabbed Melanie's hand and they made their way to the parking lot. She smiled up at him and said, "How many of your family will be there Uncle Mike?"

He grinned back and said, "I like it better when you call me Michael because you say it so soft and sweet."

"I do not say your name soft and sweet Michael Logan. Stop teasing me like that."

He looked at her with a serious expression and said, "Most of my family calls me Mike but I do love the sweet way you say my name." She didn't justify that comment with a reply.

Mrs. Logan met them at the door wearing an apron and a smile. Something about seeing her wear an apron made Melanie feel at ease because her mother used to wear an apron. The Logon clan welcomed Melanie and included her in the conversation like she was part of the family. It was a nice feeling to be part of a family again. Having Michael looking at her across the room approvingly made her feel pretty good too.

They sat down to a typical southern dinner of ham and potato salad. The group included Krystal and David, Mrs. Logan and another brother that Melanie hadn't met named Gabriel. Gabe looked a lot like Michael only a little older and not as handsome. He was visiting nearby Wilmington on business and was able to make it back to his mother's for dinner. His family was back in Charlotte where they lived. He had a wife and two sons named Jesse and Jeremiah. The boys were seven year old twins.

Melanie enjoyed the fellowship and the meal a lot more than she expected to. They didn't interrogate her with a lot of questions the way she thought they would. She even felt comfortable enough to share a little about her shop and pets. She wasn't asked about her family or any details about her past. She figured Michael must have told them she was sensitive about those subjects. She wondered what else he told them about her. Whatever it was it couldn't have been too bad because they were extremely nice to her.

Melanie had left her car at the church so Michael had to drive her back there to get it. They said their goodbyes and started walking out toward the Logan's driveway where they had left the truck. Michael stopped in the front yard and asked her if she'd like to see the tree house he and his brothers had built in the backyard when they were boys. She wasn't really in a hurry so she agreed and they went for a walk out back.

The back yard was big and there were oak trees at the back that lined what appeared to be the bank of a creek. It was a beautiful yard that looked just right for a few children to enjoy. She could just picture three little boys and a little girl playing hide and seek behind those ancient oaks. The picturesque scene made her imagine having some children playing in the backyard as she watched from the kitchen window. For some reason the little boys in her daydream bore a striking resemblance to Michael. The tree house was old but sturdy and a few boards had been nailed to the tree to form a ladder.

"I'll see you up top Michael, unless you think you're too old to climb a tree," Melanie told him as she started up the steps to the tree house.

"Who are you calling old, I'm still as nimble as a boy, " *a boy who is a lot older but I'll never admit that to her.*

Melanie had pulled herself up into the small interior of the tree house and slid over so he could join her. "This is really nice. I'll bet you guys had a lot of fun in here." Michael scooted over close to her side and said, "Those were some great times, but I spent most of my time being my brother's little slave."

She chuckled and said, "Oh that's right, you were the baby brother. Did they give you a hard time?"

He shrugged his shoulders, "no more than the usual but they didn't cut me a lot of slack back then."

"She reached over and touched his face and said, "Poor baby, do you want me to feel sorry for you?"

He grabbed her hand and held it against his face and said softly, "I do want you to feel something for me but not pity."

She took a deep breath and held his glance, "Michael, I'm not ready to talk about feelings. This is all so new and it scares me."

He released her hand and it fell back down to her side as they continued to look into each other eyes. "There's nothing to be afraid of, I'm right here beside you every step of the way."

She broke eye contact and shook her head softly. "I just have a hard time putting my trust in people especially men. Every man I ever trusted has left me when I needed them."

"Melanie I'm not going anywhere. You are going to have to trust someone, let it be me. I won't let you down."

She started moving back toward the ladder. "I really need to get home. Are you about ready to go?"

He grabbed her arm to steady her as she started down the ladder but it made her feel more nervous. "Sure let's get ourselves down out of this tree and I'll take you home."

The next week at the pet store Autumn and Melanie were feeding the animals and cleaning the cages. Autumn was beginning to open up more about her family situation. Her mother apparently had a problem with men. She was always getting involved with the wrong ones. Her parents were never married and she never knew her father. When he found out her mother was pregnant he wanted her to have an abortion. When her mother realized he wouldn't be any help to her and the baby, she left town. This was the pattern for Autumn's entire life. Her mother would move to town get a job and before long have a boyfriend. The boyfriend was usually married, an alcoholic or drug addict. She seemed to attract men with a lot of problems.

When things got to rough her mother would pack up and leave town. Autumn wanted to finish High School so she moved in with her Aunt Barb in Long Beach.

Autumn's Aunt Barb was a widow who never had children. She really seemed to want to have a good relationship with Autumn but was often critical and judgmental with her. Autumn was an independent thinker and did not respond well to criticism. This lead to a lot of misunderstandings and made home life difficult for the girl.

Autumn turned to Melanie and said, "I just want to finish School and get a place of my own."

Melanie took a minute to think and choose her words carefully, "What about college? You are so intelligent Autumn you should go to college."

Autumn shook her head, "I don't have that kind of money and my mother can barely take care of herself."

Melanie opened the door to the monkey habitat and Felix immediately jumped on her shoulder. She fed him a piece of dried fruit and replied, "There are scholarships and grants you might be able to get especially with your mother being a single parent. You can also get student loans you don't have to pay back until you get out of School. You should really consider it Autumn. I'll be glad to help you look into it. I had help with some grant money to get my business degree."

Autumn paused as she was cleaning the fish tank, her net in mid stroke, "I'll think about it. It sounds like it would be really hard."

Melanie smiled as she continued to work with Felix, "It would be as hard as working a minimum wage job with no college degree. Even if you get a little better job you're limiting your choices by not going to college. Do you want to work at a job that you hate for the rest of your life just to pay the bills?"

"I said I'll think about it and I will." With that the conversation about college was over.

Melanie hoped she had said the right things to encourage the girl. Making a living and supporting yourself alone can be tough she knew this from her own experience.

Felix the monkey was learning how to sit on Melanie's shoulder. Staying in one place was hard for him. He also had little nails that dug into her shoulder while trying to stay in place. Melanie made a pad for her shoulder so he wouldn't dig into her skin, but sometimes he started putting his little feet into her hair and playing with it. This usually resulted in her having to take it out of its usual pony tail. Her hair being very long and thick was getting to be quite a mess as she worked with him. He had it all tangled and hanging in her face.

When she looked up, Autumn started giggling. "You look like you just got out of bed after a very restless night."

"Well it will be worth it if I can teach Felix to sit in one place and not have to worry about him jumping all over the shop. You know a jumping monkey can startle some people and I don't want him the scare the customers away."

Melanie was crouching on the floor with the monkey on her shoulder trying to teach him to grab her hand and swing down, when the shop door opened and Michael walked in. She wasn't really paying attention to the customer because she was so focused on what she was doing. Michael put a finger to his lips and signaled for Autumn to be quiet and not tell Melanie he was moving up behind her. He squatted down just behind her and leaned over to whisper in her ear when Felix saw him and decided to attack. Felix considered Melanie his and didn't want another male near his territory. He jumped from Melanie's shoulder to the top of Michael's head and started screeching and jumping. Michael was so shocked that he fell back and as he fell Melanie was trying to grab the monkey and she reached forward and lost her balance. The man woman and monkey were all lying on the floor in a heap. Autumn was laughing hysterically and when Michael got over the initial shock he started laughing too.

Melanie got Felix and held him in her arms and as soon as she realized he was alright she started chuckling as well. Her hair was all over the place and her eyes were full of laughter. Michael stopped and looked at her because he had never seen such a lovely sight. He'd better keep his thoughts to himself though because she could get a little bit touchy.

"Are you okay Melanie? I hope I didn't fall on you."

"You actually broke my fall and I think I fell on you. I'm sorry Felix got upset and jumped on you. He was just protecting me because he considers me to be his territory." She smiled over at him and walked back to put the monkey back into his cage." I think he's had enough excitement for today."

Michael followed her to the back of the store and replied, "You need to explain to that monkey that he'd best make room for me in his territory or we might have a problem. I plan to be in this territory for a while."

Melanie just smiled back at him and with her hair hanging down and her beautiful smile Michael did the first thing that came to mind. He kissed her.

It was just a quick gentle kiss but it left her speechless. She didn't even think about hitting him. She thought it was nice. She wasn't about to tell him though.

"Michael Logan what was that all about? You know we are just supposed to be keeping this strictly a friendship."

"Well that was just a friendly little kiss. I had to show the monkey that this is my territory now didn't I? He grinned over at her and she couldn't really get mad at him.

"I am nobody's territory and that is not how a girl wants to be thought of"

"I don't really think of you that way, I was just trying to get a reaction out of you."

Melanie started straightening her hair and putting it back into a pony tail. "What brings you to the shop today? Can I interest you in a gerbil?"

He pointed up towards the front of the store where Autumn was arranging a pet toy display." I thought you could introduce us and maybe spend a few minutes getting acquainted. Maybe I could buy you guys some dinner."

"We have about thirty minutes until the shop closes. Do you want to hang out with us for a while?" Melanie started walking toward the front of the store.

"Autumn this is Michael Logan. He's a friend of mine that goes to my church." Michael walked over and shook hands with Autumn. "It's nice to meet you Autumn. Melanie and I were just talking about getting a bite to eat when the shop closes, would you like to join us?"

Autumn shyly shook his hand and didn't make eye contact. "I don't want to horn in on your date. Three's a crowd you know."

Melanie shook her head and walked over closer to the girl. "The Father, Son and Holy Ghost are three and they always want company. Michael and I would love to have you join us. He is the leader of the youth group at church I told you about and this would not be a date. We're just friends"

Autumn hesitated for a few seconds and seemed to weigh the decision. Going home to her Aunt's house held little appeal. "Make it pizza and you're on." The girl looked a little apprehensive about being with a couple of old folks but she was willing. Michael grinned that little grin Melanie couldn't resist. "Pizza it is then. Now what else do you ladies need to do here before you can close up?"

They settled the animals down for the night and counted the cash drawer. Melanie put the money in the safe and it was time to close the shop. As she was getting ready to lock the door, a young man pulled up in an older model Honda and jumped out and came running up to the door of the shop. "Are you still open? I need to get a tropical fish for my little sister right away before she realizes her fish died today."

Melanie let him in and showed him to the fish tank helping him choose a fish that would be the exact replica of the dearly departed. "Hey Mike, what are you doing here?"

Michael went over and shook the young man's hand. "What's going on Chad? We've been missing you at the youth meetings."

Chad look embarrassed as he looked back over at Michael. "Things at home are a little hard right now. My little sister had been diagnosed with leukemia. We haven't really told anyone at the church about it yet."

Michael reached over and put a hand on the boys shoulder, "Hey that tough news Chad. Is there anything we can do to help your family?"

"We really are just taking it day by day right now. We aren't sure what her treatment will be yet."

Melanie got the selected fish in the net and deposited him into a bag of water and handed it to Chad. "Please take this fish at no charge. It's the least I can do." He looked at her in surprise, "But you don't even know us." He tried to give her the fish back.

She just smiled and continued to push the fish into his hand. "You take this fish young man and I don't want to hear another thing about it."

"Yes Mam. Thank you for staying open and getting the fish for Gina." He started toward the door to leave.

"You are most welcome. Come back and see us again." He looked back at Autumn and nodded his head in her direction, "I think I just might do that."

They went to dinner at the local pizza restaurant. Between the two of them Michael and Melanie had Autumn feeling at ease in a short time. They shared the story of how they met and she laughed out loud at Melanie's description of the big scary man that came to her rescue. Before the evening was over Michael had her promise to go to the next youth meeting. She did have one condition and that was that Melanie had to go with her. Melanie agreed and Michael grinned. Mission accomplished, not only had Autumn agreed to try the youth group, but Melanie was going to come as well. As soon as she met those kids she would be a goner. God was in control.

Chapter Seven

Melanie woke up with a heavy weight on her chest. She felt a little shortness of breath and wondered what was wrong with her. Then the weight moved and she realized it was Lancelot her cat sleeping on top of her. She stretched her arms out from under the covers and moved the cat over to the other side of the bed. Newman lay sleeping at the foot of the bed and Pepe' was asleep under the edge of the covers, so much for training the boys to sleep alone. She has spoiled them for too long. When her mother had died and her brother left she found great comfort in having her pets in bed with her; especially on those long lonely nights when she couldn't sleep and couldn't stop weeping for the loss of her mother. She was paying the price for that companionship now because she couldn't roll over in her own bed without squishing a cat.

The shop was closed today and she planed to get some work done in her yard. The cold weather was almost over and it was time to start clearing and planning for her shrubbery and flower garden. Not knowing about which plants grew best in the sandy soil, Helen her next door neighbor had kindly agreed to help with the planning.

Helen had become a valued neighbor and friend. She had wisdom that could only come from experience. Melanie hoped she would get a chance to talk to Helen about the thing that was uppermost in her mind which is Michael and if she should become more involved with him by working with the youth group. She has been praying about the situation but her emotions are so confused when it came to Michael that she was not sure what she should do.

Helen's dog, Peaches the cocker spaniel got along great with the boys. In fact Pepe', who seemed to think he's a large dog had developed a crush on Peaches. He followed her around the yard and watched her like a love starved puppy. He didn't seem to realize she was at least four times his size .Love, it seemed, truly was blind and kind of stupid too.

Yesterday as Melanie let Pepe' out into the back yard to exercise, he saw Peaches next door in her back yard. Even though he was inside the fence, he followed her along the fence line whining while walking back and forth as she played with her ball. He kept on until his whining picked up intensity and volume. It sounded like a chorus of sick puppies crying for their mother. It was sad. Pepe' had it bad for Peaches. This relationship doesn't stand a chance.

Newman had made a wonderful discovery. It seemed the sandy soil of the coast has some entertaining creatures. He spent the better part of a whole day discovering the wonder of a cute little green lizard. The little guy would zip under the porch and Newman would dig him out. The little green guy would run up the side of a tree and Newman would follow him right up to the top. It's a wonder that the little lizard didn't have a heart attack. Newman wouldn't hurt him. He had been around enough other animals to learn not to do anything to endanger them. I guess the lizard didn't want to take any chances.

Today it seemed that Newman had discovered some type of sand crab. It burrowed into the sand and hid. He hasn't figured out how to find the tiny crab after he made his disappearance. The sand crabs in Long Beach are safe from Newman the explorer today. He has found a new form of entertainment. As Melanie dug in the sandy soil to prepare it for planting, he was hypnotized by the movement of the sand flying through the air. Sometimes his little brain just can't wrap itself around how these things happen.

Just as he was settling in on the side lines to watch this mysterious phenomenon, Helen came through the fence with Peaches. Even though Newman had met Peaches, he wasn't taking any chances so he moved himself over to the safety of the deck railing.

"Good morning dear, such a nice day for working in the yard. How are things going so far?" Helen was sporting a large straw hat that had large colorful ribbons and a patch of flowers that were woven into them. It was orange and green with pink flowers and quite a colorful sight for first thing in the morning.

Melanie put the hoe down and went over toward Helen, "So far so good I guess. I am still not sure what I want to plant back here but I know which areas need something. I thought I could break up the soil and fertilize the areas I know will be getting some new plants."

The two ladies moved over to the deck and shared a cup of coffee as Helen explained the types of plants that would do well in this area. It didn't take long for the two ladies to have a definite plan for exactly what Melanie's yard would look like in the spring. Melanie had dreamed of having her own house and yard for so long. Now that she had the opportunity, she wanted to make the yard as pretty as she could. She had always believed a pretty yard with flowers, trees and shrubs, planted in the right places, framed a house and made it seem more welcoming.

After they worked in the yard for a while Melanie prepared a cold drink for them to share on the deck. The conversation between them flowed so naturally that it seemed like they had been friends for years. Melanie felt as soon as they met, she and Helen had a strong connection and her instincts turned out to be right. Helen began to talk about her husband.

"George and I used to work out in the yard together. In the spring we would plant our flowers and vegetables and in the fall we would mulch and prepare the ground for the next spring. The summer was a time to enjoy our fresh tomatoes and beans. In the winter we would sit by the fire and read our garden books. In those last years that we had together, each new season was a cause for celebration. The gardening gave us an opportunity to celebrate each time George made it through another season. At first we worked together but when he got too weak to help, he sat outside and watched me work. It was a sad and happy time. Sad because our time was growing short but happy because we had another day together."

Melanie turned to Helen and asked the question that burned in her heart, "Did you decide after living through that pain, you could never take the chance of loving again?"

Helen chose her words carefully for she realized how much Melanie was struggling with her own feelings, "Do you wish that you'd never known your mother?"

Melanie did not hesitate, "Of course not. The years that I spent with my family were the best. We had hard times but we had an abundance of love."

Helen just looked at her a minute as she turned the thought over in her head, "Melanie we were put here on this earth by our creator to have an impact on others. If we never give others love, how can we be like our Father? Without love where is the meaning for our life?"

Melanie shook her head, "But you don't understand Helen, I do love other people. I know God tells us to love one another. I love my brother and I love the children I teach and I love my animals more than I like most people. It's just men I don't trust. Most men that I have known in my life have not been reliable. Even my former pastor didn't stand up for me when the other members wanted me to stop teaching their children."

Helen was silent for a few seconds and then she said the words that burned in Melanie's heart, "Jesus was a man Melanie, and he is the only one any of us can depend on. The truth is that most people will let you down from time to time because they are human and have a sinful nature. If you're looking for a perfect man there isn't going to be one out there for you. Don't be afraid to experience life because you never will know the fullness of your joy unless you experience a little pain."

Melanie crinkled up her face and said, "I think I'd rather keep on an even path without all those highs and lows. I just don't think I can go through the pain of losing somebody else I love."

Helen just smiled because she knew that Melanie couldn't control her feelings that way. "Love has a way of sneaking up on you when you're not looking. Before you know it, your right in the middle of it and it's too late to turn back."

Melanie thought of Michael and dismissed the thought. She would not let herself develop feelings for Michael Logan. That was not in her plan and it was the last thing she wanted to happen.

At the same time that Melanie was making this resolve, Michael Logan was spending some time over at his mother's house helping her put some things in the attic. Mrs. Logan had decided to purchase new bedroom furniture and wanted to move her old set to the attic. The old bedroom furniture had been in his parent's room for many years. He understood why his mother didn't want to part with it even though it had long ago gone out of style and was showing signs of the years of wear. Getting the furniture up the attic stairs was a challenge for him. The pieces might be old but were made of sturdy wood that was pretty heavy. As he carried each piece he thought of his parent's marriage and how much in love they were for so many years. He had made a resolve within himself that he would not settle for less than the type of love his parents had.

He had prayed and waited for a long time for the right woman to come into his life. When he first saw Melanie with her silly pajamas and her obvious devotion to that cat, something struck him and he knew this was the woman that he had been waiting for. It wasn't anything that she said or did exactly, or not even her quirky brand of humor that he enjoyed so much. It was a feeling deep inside that told him this was his mate. After much prayer and consideration Michael still believed that Melanie was the one for him. The problem was Melanie had been so beaten up by life that he was afraid the love of his life might pass him by because of her deep rooted wound of fear. He whispered yet another prayer for her emotional healing and finished the job at hand. Daydreaming was not going to get this furniture moved.

Michael had just gotten the final piece up the attic stairs so he came back downstairs and joined his mother in the kitchen. "Do you have any of those cookies I like in the pantry, mom?"

She went over to get his cookies and poured him a glass of milk. She looked over at him with a playful grin and said, "What would your Melanie think if she saw you sitting here in your mom's kitchen having cookies and milk like you did when you were a little boy?"

His face got serious as he thoughtfully took a bite of his cookie, "Mom I know that I told you when I met her she is the one that God has for me, but she doesn't seem to be interested in a relationship. I'm just not sure how to handle things with her. She seems to like me one day and ignores me the next day. It's really driving me crazy.'

Mrs. Logan chuckled, "Mike that girl has feelings for you she just isn't ready to admit it. I saw the way she looked at you. You told me yourself she had a hard time trusting people, you just have to be patient and gentle with her."

"You know that patience is not one of the things that the good Lord gifted me with. I want to know I have a chance with her. I want to spend time getting to know her better without having to watch every thing I say because I might scare her off."

"Just spend some time in prayer about it Mike. You know the Lord tells us if we lack wisdom to ask it of him. I'd say you could use a little wisdom in this situation."

He rose to leave and she walked him to the door. Just pray for me Mom. I have been waiting for a long time for the right woman and I don't want to blow it now." She hugged him and replied, "Honey put it all in God's hands. He knows what's best for you and Melanie. You have to trust him with your whole life and that includes matters of the heart."

Michael decided to just causally ride by Melanie's house and see if she might be at home. He knew her shop was closed today but she hadn't told him about any plans that she might have. She wasn't in the habit of sharing her plans with him. This was yet another frustrating thing for Michael to handle. He just wanted to make sure she didn't need help with anything. Her little car could break down again or she might need help with something at her house. She told him herself she didn't know many people in town. He wanted to be there if she should need anything. Now the only problem was to get her to admit she might need his help.

Michael drove slowly down Melanie's street a couple of times. It took his second pass by the house to see she was working in the yard.

He was on his third trip down her street when he realized how silly he was acting and pulled up into her driveway. He got out of his truck and walked behind the house and spotted Melanie up to her knees in dirt digging some type of hole near the corner of her yard. The little dog began to bark at him and then she turned around and saw him and smiled. Boy Michael thought; *I sure would love to have that smile great me at the beginning of each new day.*

Melanie tried to wipe the dirt from her hands on the leg of her pants, "Hey Michael, how are you? I wish you would have gotten here an hour earlier. I would have put you to work. I'm getting my yard ready for spring planting. I'm so excited, I've got it all planned just the way I want it." Her face was flushed from exertion and she had such a joyful look about her that Michael didn't answer her for a minute.

"I'd be glad to help you now if I can. What else needs to be done?"

Michael found out something new about Melanie in the next two hours. She was a hard worker. They broke the ground and fertilized several large areas in her yard. One was for vegetables and one was for flowers. Then there were several sites where she planned to put in dogwoods and azalea bushes. Holes were dug and potting soil and fertilizer was added. While they worked, Melanie shared her vision for the yard with him. She took such pleasure in the work that Michael enjoyed it too. Just being with her made him happy.

When they were finished Melanie brought some cold iced tea out to the deck and they sat out there and just rested quietly for a few minutes. Some people don't appreciate the companionship found in working together. Apparently Michael understood this principle and Melanie was secretly pleased. She ended up being the one to break the silence.

"Thank you for helping me with this Michael. It would have taken me much longer without your help. I guess you figured out that I want to make my yard bloom with color this spring."

He took a drink from his glass and looked over at her, "I was glad to help. I hope you'll feel free to call me anytime you need help with your place. You still have my phone number don't you?"

She just grinned at him, "My Momma always told me a woman shouldn't chase after a man and that includes calling him. I am used to taking care of myself, I'll be fine."

He leaned toward her over the table and grabbed her hand. "I want you to promise me that if you need any help you will call. I know you don't know many people here and I will not think you're chasing me, I know better than that."

"Okay I will put your number in my speed dial and if I have an emergency I'll call you first." She didn't think for a minute it was likely to happen.

Chapter Eight

Melanie remembered hearing her sweet Aunt Rose saying, "Never say never." This morning she might have to eat her words about never asking Michael for help. There was water gushing out of the wall in the bathroom like a geyser and the floor already had two inches of water in the bathroom and the hall. She had no idea how to turn the water off. If she didn't get some help and fast all her floors and carpets would be ruined. Her living room furniture would not survive a flood either. She made a fast decision. Pride was one thing but being practical was another. She pushed four on her speed dial.

Michael was drinking his morning coffee when the phone rang. He had just finished his morning prayer and Bible study. He had given his relationship with Melanie over to God. He was not going to worry about it. If God wanted them together then he would make a way. He felt so peaceful having made that decision and all of the sudden the phone rang

"Hello Michael, its Melanie. I need your help. I have a broken water pipe or something and it's flooding my house. Can you come right away?" Her words were anxious and rushed.

He smiled as he told Melanie that he would be right over. I guess God was making a way.

When Michael arrived five minutes later he was greeted by a soggy Melanie and three soggy animals. The cats had taken refuge on the back of the living room sofa. The little dog was splashing around in the water barking at it as if his barking could make the water stop.

Michael went to the back yard and turned the water valve off to the house right away. Melanie was looking very relieved. Her hall fortunately led to the kitchen so the water hadn't reached her carpet or living room furniture.

"Thank you so much for coming. I was thinking about moving my furniture to higher ground." She looked deflated and worried about her house.

"Let me take a look in the bathroom where the water was leaking and I'll see if I can fix the problem." He started splashing down the hall with her right on his heels.

"I can call a plumber if I need to Michael, I just didn't know how to shut the water off." She was relieved he got the water to stop and really glad that he came right over. She frowned a little when she thought she would owe him a big favor.

"Honey, I'm a general contractor, I think I can fix a little leak for you. Let me grab some tools from the truck."

"It was hardly a little leak. It was more like Niagara Falls." She followed him back through the house and watched him as he got a tool box from behind the seat of his truck.

When he came back inside he said, "Why don't you get some towels or something and try to clean some of this water up. If you can keep it from going any further into the living room I think it will clean up fine. I have a shop vacuum at home I'll bring over to help clean up your mess. It will pick up the water pooled on the floor."

In his take charge fashion Michael was as good as his word, he had the pipe leading to the water heater fixed within an hour and then he went and got the industrial shop vacuum and helped her clean up the water in the house. Melanie had changed clothes and was making a fresh pot of coffee when he was finishing up.

"Michael do I owe you anything for all your hard work?"

"Why don't you come to dinner with me and we'll call it even?"

She thought about everything he had done for her this morning and wanted to do something nice for him in return. "If you can be here at 7:30 this evening I'll cook your dinner. Do you like southern fried chicken and cold slaw?" Fried chicken was her specialty. She didn't know how to cook all the new healthy foods that were popular but she had a feeling Michael might appreciate fried chicken.

Michael was very pleased with this development because he had not been invited past the front door of her house before today. "I love fried chicken and I will be here tonight at 7:30 with bells on. Would you like for me to bring anything?"

She shook her head, "I'll take care of the meal. You just show up and remember to mind your manners while you're here."

"Miss Melanie, have I ever given you a reason to believe you should be afraid to be alone with me?" He wanted her to realize she could trust him.

She thought about it and saw how she was judging him by her past experiences again. "No, I am not afraid of being alone with you. We're alone right now aren't we?" But if she were to be truthful with herself, she was afraid to be alone with him. Not afraid of him doing anything improper but afraid of the feelings she had when they were together.

Michael walked to the door and gave her a look that made her feel like he was looking into her heart. "I'll see you tonight then."

Melanie was glad to have her house back in order. She sat back down with her coffee and made plans for her dinner with Michael. If she had called a plumber, by the time he got there a lot of her things would have been ruined. It was nice to have someone to call in an emergency. She missed having her brother nearby. She had gotten a letter from him yesterday and had put it away to read later. She got the letter from her bedroom and opened it and began to read.

Dear Mel,

I know it's been a while since I wrote to you. Sometimes I have a hard time thinking of you and home. I miss you and wish we could be together again. I am happy for you that you are starting a new life. The pet shop sounds great and I wish I could see it. I want you to have a good life and I want all your dreams to come true.

My wife Rachel has filed for divorce. It is so hard for me to think of her after all we have been through. I suppose it is for the best so she can get on with her life. I hear she has gone into rehab and gotten off the stuff. Maybe she can have a good life too. I guess her life will be without me. At least she is out there instead of in here.

This place is like a different world. I have been trying to figure out how men learn to survive. I think they just pass the time in meaningless ways waiting for another chance at life outside these walls. At least that is what I have been doing. You'll be pleased to know that I have been going to chapel on Sundays. It is a diversion for many of us and I like the guy who comes to teach the Bible. He is a former inmate and he has turned himself around. This makes me believe I might have the chance one day to turn myself around.

Our father has come to visit me a couple of times. I can't figure out why after all these years he wants to see me but I talk to him because he comes and visitors are rare. He still says he was looking for us after mom threw him out and that her family wouldn't tell him where we were. He goes on and on about how he wanted to see us and wondered where we were and if we were alright. I don't know if I can believe him because it seems to be going against Momma. I don't know what I think but he does seem to care about me now, so I guess that's something. Why don't you talk to him again and see what you think? He is the only parent we have left.

Thank you for the packages you send with the things you think I might need. I especially liked the books. How are the cats and the mutt doing? I hope they are keeping you company. You shouldn't be alone Mel. You need to get married and have children. You were like a mother to me at times and you were really good at it. I love you and wish you all the best.

Jerry

Melanie put the letter down as the tears fell down her face. Her baby brother was in jail and would be there for a long time. How it broke her heart. She wondered if she had been a better sister to him, she could have done something to keep him from ending up there. She can't seem to forgive herself. Feeling responsible for Jerry had been a part of her life for so long that she couldn't stop. She knew in her heart he made the choices that led him to this trouble but she couldn't stand to think of all those wasted years. Eighteen years is a long time to a twenty five year old. She knew that some prisoners get out early for good behavior but she doesn't really know how much time could be taken off the sentence. When she heard the verdict she couldn't bring herself to meet with his attorney again.

Melanie thought about what Jerry said about their father. She was glad he was going to see Jerry if he wanted to see him. Maybe it was a sign that he does care. She just doesn't trust him very much. Why would her Momma tell her that he didn't want to see them if he did? Would she do that knowing how much she and Jerry missed their father? The truth was that her Momma was a bitter woman after her husband left. She could have lied to them about what happened. Melanie knew that if her mother was lying she should give her father a chance to explain. How could she know for sure? The only person besides her Momma who knew what really happened would be Aunt Rose.

Melanie decided to write to her Aunt Rose and ask her about her parents divorce. She prayed God would reveal the truth to her and Jerry. It seemed so strange to her to be able to think of her father as a good man and not the selfish cruel man her mother told them about so often. Melanie realized the very fact that her mother spoke so harshly of her father was wrong. Why say such things to children who are missing their father? Was her Momma really the selfish one? It was very hard for her to think of her dead mother that way. This whole matter would require a lot of prayer.

The day went by quickly and before Melanie had time to pray about her father, it was time for her dinner with Michael. She had been busy all day and after work she had to hurry home to start the meal. She wanted to make a special dessert that had to chill for at least an hour. Her chicken was ready and so was her potato salad but she wasn't, so she would have to set the table after she took a shower. She wanted to have time to work on her wild hair. She knew Michael liked it hanging down on her shoulders instead of pulled back and it took some time to tame it enough to wear it like that.

She was out of the shower and debating about what to wear when the door bell rang. He better not be fifteen minutes early or she might have to hurt him. She peeked out her front window and saw his truck in the driveway and groaned. He was early and right this minute as she was standing there in her robe, he was waiting on the doorsteps.

What should she do she wondered? She went to the door and shouted, "Michael Logan you are early. You said seven thirty sharp. I am not ready yet. Come back in ten minutes."

He rang the bell again for effect, "Melanie honey that's silly. Why don't you let me in and I'll wait inside where it's warm." He really didn't mind waiting but couldn't pass up the opportunity to tease her. "You know it's a little cool out here tonight. I might catch a chill and get sick standing out here."

Melanie didn't answer him; she was frantically trying to throw her clothes on as fast as possible. She had decided to wear a pair of casual black slacks and a red knit blouse. She was pulling the blouse over her head as she stood behind the closed door and answered, "You're a big tough man aren't you? A little chill wouldn't get you down. Maybe you should stay out there a while longer and see." She pulled the door open and grinned at him. He noticed how her hair was a little wild and her blouse was a little crooked and he grinned back.

"Well you might as well come in and get out of the cold then," as she motioned for him to come in. She didn't exactly sound thrilled about it.

"I'm sorry I was a little early, Melanie. I didn't mean to get you all in a dither." He was chucking under his breath because he saw she was embarrassed.

"I am not in a dither whatever that means; I am just not quite ready yet. You can have a seat and I'll be back shortly." She walked back upstairs to finish getting ready and he went into the living room and sat down.

As soon as he sat on the couch, Newman jumped up on his lap demanding attention. Michael scratched the big orange cat around the ears and he started purring loudly. Lancelot was eyeing them from his perch on the chair nearby. He was looking at Newman with a disgusted look as if to say he was a pushover. He slowly made his way over to the couch and looked at Michael and let out a loud "meow." He stared at Michael as if waiting for him to respond and loudly meowed again for good measure. "Do you want me to scratch your ears too old fella?" Michael reached over to pat Lance on the head and the cat started walking in the other direction just to let the man know he was not a pushover like Newman. Michael reached over and picked him up. "You remember me I'm the knight who rescued your lady in distress." Lance must have decided he was going to be friends because he let Michael settle him on the couch beside him and rub his back softly.

Melanie happened to be watching them from the stairs and she had heard the knight and lady comment. "So do you consider yourself my knight in shining armor now?"

Michael was clearly embarrassed to have been overheard talking to the cat. "Well it seemed like something that a cat named Lancelot would want to hear."

Melanie chuckled, "I guess you were appealing to his knightly side." She came into the room and sat down on the couch on the other side of the cat. "I never asked you how you feel about cats. Some men don't like them."

Michael continued to stroke the cats, "I've always liked animals and cats are no exception. I think cats are very honest animals. They either like you or they don't and they let you know what they want." Melanie considered his comment, "You could really say the same thing about dogs and children."

Michael reached over the cat and brushed her hair back with his hand, "I think I could safely say that would apply to you too. You tell me what you think and let me know what you want. I like the way you are honest and direct."

She tucked some more hair behind her ear, "I guess that comes from my West Virginia upbringing. Most of our family was what you might consider mountain people and they had a very direct manner about them. I think it is the best way to deal with people. Doesn't the Bible say if thy brother offends thee go to him? Telling other people when about something bothers me is a waste of time and energy."

"So Melanie tell me honestly", he paused to make her wonder at his next words, "When do we eat because I smell something that is making me hungry." He didn't want to hear too much honesty tonight. His poor old heart couldn't take it.

She got up and walked toward the kitchen, "If you'll help set the table we can eat pretty soon. The dishes are in that cabinet to your right." She pointed to the correct cabinet and started getting the food out to take into the dining room.

The meal turned out well despite the fact Melanie was rushed. The dessert of apricots and a creamy sauce was a big hit. Melanie was pleased because this was the first time she had anyone over to dinner at her new house.

"Did you enjoy your dinner Michael? I really wanted to make something I thought you might like. "

"I really enjoyed it. Everything was good, thank you for inviting me." He settled back in his chair.

"You are my first dinner guest since I moved here. I hope to be able to entertain more often when I get settled."

"And I hope to be included in some of those plans of yours."

Melanie got up from the table and started clearing the dishes. "Why don't you relax in the other room and I'll clean up?"

Michael rose and picked up a serving dish, "Why don't you relax and I'll clean up?" He looked over at her and grinned.

She shook her head, not wanting to let him have the upper hand. "I'll let you help if you're a good boy."

He started walking in the direction of the kitchen, "I am on my best behavior tonight, can't you tell?"

She started stacking the dishes in the sink, "Your best behavior should not include being early and teasing me for not being ready."

He handed her a serving dish, "I know but you have to admit, it was a perfect opportunity for a little teasing."

She got quiet as she started placing the dishes in the dishwasher. She had spotted the opened letter from Jerry she had put on the shelf with her other mail. She couldn't help but feel sad that he couldn't have been here tonight. She wished she could share her little house by the sea with him. She wished he could meet Michael and tell her what he thought of him.

Michael came up behind her and touched her on the shoulder to get her attention, "What's the matter, honey?" He turned her around and looked into her eyes with sincere concern, "Why do you look so sad all of the sudden?"

She considered the possibility of lying to him but she didn't want to be dishonest. "I got a letter from my brother today. I just wish he could be here with me, I miss him so much."

Michael turned her around and put his arms around her. "I'm sorry honey; I know it must be hard for you."

She laid her head on his broad shoulder and gave in to the tears she had been holding back. "Sometimes it feels like I have lost everyone I ever loved. I know Jerry isn't dead but I have lost his presence in my life just the same. My mother is gone and now my father has shown up to complicate things. I have a lot of baggage Michael. You might want to reconsider being my friend."

He patted her back gently wishing he could take her pain on himself. "Melanie, I want to be more than your friend, I've told you that. I want to be the one to help you sort out your baggage. I will do whatever I can to help you through this."

She sniffed and started wiping the tears from her face. "I'm sorry. I'm really not the type of woman who cries over every little thing. Thanks for the shoulder though."

"Anytime Melanie, just call on me your knight in shining armor." She laughed gently, "Don't get carried away Michael. I am an independent woman. I just had a couple of weak moments. Don't get used to the rescue routine."

He grinned that little boy grin, "I wouldn't think of it, Melanie. How about you're coming to my rescue?"

"What are you talking about Michael?" I don't see you need rescuing."

"I am talking about the youth group. I need some help tomorrow with a fund-raiser. My assistant has backed out and parent participation is almost non existent. How about coming over to the church tomorrow and washing a few cars?"

Chapter Nine

On Saturday morning Melanie had to go the shop to check on Autumn to talk to her about working by herself in the store so she could help with the youth's car wash. The animals had to be cared for and the cages cleaned. Melanie also wanted to check on Felix. He had made such progress that she considered taking him with her to the car wash. He could help draw customers and maybe hold something to put the money in. She wasn't sure how he would react to a large group of kids though. It might upset him and make him hard to control in public.

Melanie went over to his habitat and opened the door. Felix immediately jumped on her shoulder. Melanie had trained him not to dig her shoulder with his little claws and she could carry him on her shoulder without wearing the padding now. He had been out on a couple short outings with her wearing his leash and harness. He attracted a lot of attention in public and she wanted him to get used to being around more people. He had learned to retrieve small items for her and without any real prompting from Melanie had struck up a friendship with Pepe'.

They seemed to enjoy each others company whenever Melanie brought the dog to the shop. Felix seemed to like the idea of another animal that was smaller than he. He would try to groom Pepe' and the dog didn't seem to mind the attention. It was a rather comical sight though the monkey and the Chihuahua stretched out on the floor beside each other just chilling. Both animals were rather high strung and energetic so seeing them so relaxed with each other was unusual.

Melanie and Autumn discussed it, and agreed that Melanie would go over to the church for four hours and then come back and relieve Autumn at the store. Melanie trusted the girl to take care of things but it was hard for her to leave the shop on a Saturday which was usually her busiest day of the week. The people have come to expect to see her and she didn't want to disappoint them.

Melanie drove over to the church and saw the signs on the way advertising the car wash. She was anxious to meet some of the teens since she had heard so much about them from Michael. She had met a couple of the boys at church on youth Sunday. The praise band had been so awesome she had to go over and compliment them. She hadn't really met any of the girls. She had been praying about becoming involved with these kids and she really wasn't sure if she should. The fact that Michael was their youth leader could make things uncomfortable for her if their friendship didn't work out. He seemed to want much more than a friendship and she didn't feel that she could handle a relationship with him. He seemed to think they already have a relationship and that really worried her.

The kids were gathered in the parking lot with their buckets and hoses already working on a couple of cars. The church members will most likely support them today by bringing their cars to be washed. Melanie got out of her car and started walking in their direction. She looked like one of the kids in her jeans and her hair in a pony tail. She came up behind Michael and startled him by tapping him on the shoulder. He was hard at work polishing the hood of an SUV.

Michael jumped like he had experienced an electric shock. He knew it had to be Melanie because nothing else felt like the jolt he felt when she touched him. He turned around and smiled at her. "Hey Melanie, are you ready to wash some cars?"

She put her hand to her head in a sassy salute, "Yes sir, reporting for duty, sir."

The two young men who were working on the car with Michael stopped and were watching them.

"Chad, Mark, this is Melanie Byron. She is a new member at our church who has a little experience dealing with kids. She came to help us out today."

Melanie shook hands with the boys and Michael took her around and introduced her to the rest of the group. They seemed to accept her without question and the next two hours, everyone was very busy washing cars. They formed a girl and a boy team and the cars formed two lines. Both lines were kept busy with washing cars for a couple hours straight and seemed to be running out of steam. It was obvious the kids needed a break. The church had furnished bag lunches that they would eat in the fellowship hall.

Melanie wanted to discuss how they would handle the lunch process so she walked over to the boy's line to talk to Michael. She forgot that she still had a large sponge in her hand. Chad, one of the boys pointed at her hand and started laughing. "Do you think Mr. Mike needs to be washed up, Miss Melanie?" She couldn't pass up the opportunity to tease Michael. She held the sponge up and moved it close to his face. "He does have a smudge of dirt right there" and she gently touched the sponge to his face.

He grinned a bad boy grin as he grabbed her arm and brought her body closer to his so the kids couldn't hear his reply. "You better not start something you can't finish."

She pulled back from him and took the sponge away from his face. She kept her voice low so that it wouldn't carry far, "You'd better behave before you give the kids the wrong idea." He looked around at all the faces watching them and realized he needed to be on his guard with Melanie so near and these kids watching their every move. He moved a little further away from her and spoke loud enough for the kids to hear, "So what are we going to do about lunch?"

Melanie relaxed a little because she felt a little surge of electricity when they got close enough to touch. "I thought we could go in shifts, the girls could go first while the boys hold down the fort and then we could stay here while you guys go." Michael looked over at the tired looking girls and shook his head in agreement. One of the boys looked like he was going to object but Michael stopped him with a look.

The car wash turned out to be a great success. One thing Melanie realized was she loved the challenge of teenagers. One of the girls confided to her about how hard it was for the girls to stay home when the boys went to the gulf. They wanted someone who would be their leader that would have the time and energy to do the mission trips and fund raisers and all the fun activities they had. There was a Christian concert in a month and the girls wanted her to go and be their chaperone. She told them she would see what she could do but she couldn't see herself disappointing them. She had even thought of the possibility of Autumn coming along.

Melanie knew she could be the leader that these girls wanted and needed. The only problem that held her back was Michael. What will she do about her budding feelings for him and his obvious feelings for her? She found herself feeling the need to spend some serious time in prayer. The move and the business had taken up so much of her time. She needed to get her priorities straight and get God back in the driver's seat.

Back at the shop there had been a little mishap in Melanie's absence. Felix had escaped from his habitat and had managed to open the cat cage where four kittens had escaped. He was trying to open the puppy cage when Autumn saw a kitten scurry up behind the cash register counter as she was ringing up a lady's order. The lady didn't seem to notice the kitten but Autumn knew something was up. As soon as she walked to the back of the store, she saw Felix hard at work on the latch of the puppy cage. Autumn had not handled Felix very much because Melanie had been spending a lot of time with his training. When she reached out to try to pick him up, he started chattering and jumped on top of the cages. Autumn ignored him and started trying to recapture the four kittens that were loose in the store. She really hated to call Melanie but knew she needed help. If a customer opened the door to come in, Felix or one of the kittens might get outside to the parking lot. That could spell disaster. Autumn dialed Melanie's cell phone number.

Melanie heard her cell phone ring in her purse over by her car. She ran over to answer it. Only a couple of people had her number so she knew it might be Autumn calling from the shop. She picked up the phone and Autumn filled her in on what had happened. Amber, one of the teenage girls was standing nearby and had heard her side of the conversation. When Melanie hung up Amber came over to her, "Ill come with you and help if I can." Melanie, who was hurriedly getting her things, agreed. "I'll just talk to Michael and let him know I have to leave. Michael, who was in the fellowship hall having his lunch with the boys, rose when he saw her coming.

The number of cars had dwindled down a good bit and it would be easy for them to handle things without Melanie and Amber. "Michael, there's a little problem at the shop. I have to leave. Amber wants to come with me and I'll see that she gets home. Can you handle things here?"

Michael could see by the look on her face she was concerned, "Sure, we'll be fine. I'll call you later and you can fill me in." She had already turned to go, "That sounds good, and I'll talk to you later."

As she walked away Michael noticed she was almost eager for him to call later. Since her guard was down, she hadn't had time to tell herself it was a bad idea for them to start talking on the phone. He was pleased with the way the day had gone. Melanie took to the kids like a duck to water and they seemed to really like her. It had already been suggested to him by a couple of the kids that she accompany them to the concert later in the month. The youth group could sure use her help, but that's not the main reason that Michael wanted her involved.

The truth was that he had his own selfish reason. He wanted to be able to spend more time with her. Was he trying to put his own wants ahead of the good of the group? He had wanted to kiss her today when they were playing with the sponge. Who was he kidding? He wanted to kiss her anytime she was nearby. "Lord, don't let me mess this up. I want to be used as a leader to these teenagers, but I also want to pursue a personal relationship with Melanie. Can it all work out at the same time? It's going to take your hand Lord, help me to take my hands off this situation."

Melanie and Amber got to the pet shop in record time. Autumn had managed to catch two of the four kittens. Felix was still acting hyper and jumping around from the top of one cage to another.

Melanie went directly back to him and started talking to him in a calm voice to coax him to come to her. It only took her about ten minutes to get him calm enough to be held and she soothed him for a few more minutes before she put him in his habitat. By that time the girls had rounded up the two other kittens and were putting them back into their cage too. The craziness was calm in about fifteen minutes.

Autumn started to apologize to Melanie, "I don't know how he got out, and he was fine the last time I was back here showing some people the puppies." Melanie laid her hand on Autumn's shoulder to reassure her, it wasn't your fault, and I had him out this morning remember? I must not have made sure the latch was secure. How did you figure out that he was loose?"

Autumn shared the story of the little kitten scooting behind the counter and they all laughed. Melanie turned to the girls and thought this could be an opportunity for Autumn to make a friend. "Autumn, this is Amber from the youth group at church. She came back with me to help." The girls looked at each other and smiled. Amber found her voice first, "We kind of met while we were catching the kittens. Is it always this exciting around here? What a fun job." Autumn seemed at ease, "I was very happy Melanie hired me. It's fun working here. The animals are great and Melanie is the best boss I ever had."

Melanie smiled at them as she made her way back up front, "How many bosses have you had all together?" Autumn looked a little embarrassed, "Well only two but you are by far the best. Melanie turned around and looked back at the girls, "Thanks, I think that was a compliment."

The rest of the day at the shop went by quickly. Amber decided to stay and hang out after calling and getting permission from her mother. The three of them were going to get something to eat after they closed the shop. Melanie thought Amber would be a good influence on Autumn if they could get better acquainted.

They closed up and went out for burgers and milkshakes. It was a fun time for Autumn. She and Amber seem to be getting along well. While they were sitting at the restaurant, Amber brought up the subject of church and the youth group. "Autumn you really should come to church with us and join our youth group. We have such a good time and Melanie might even become one of our teachers." Both pairs of eyes rested on Melanie's face and she felt cornered. "Well I haven't decided for sure, but I am praying about it."

Amber looked at Melanie with eyes that looked older and wiser than her sixteen years. "You like Mr. Mike don't you? Is that why you don't want to be our teacher? That just makes it better because you can spend a lot of time with him." Melanie was shaking her head before the girl had finished her sentence, "Michael and I are just friends. It wouldn't be appropriate for us to be teachers together if we were anything else."

Amber frowned back at her, "Well why not? You're both single aren't you? Mr. Mike is a great guy. You should give him a chance."

Melanie was thinking about what Amber said later when she was at home. Michael was a great guy. What was it that scared her so much about dating him? It's the strong way she felt inside. He could really hurt her if they started seeing each other and then it didn't work out. She can't begin to imagine how much it would hurt if he left her. It would hurt right now.

"Lord is Helen right? Is love worth a chance?" Melanie wasn't convinced. She knew she had to resolve her mixed up feeling about men. Those feelings started when her father left. Maybe she should write him and see if he wants to come visit her. She couldn't believe she was even considering doing it but she was. She wished she had someone to talk to about all this. Michael crossed her mind as a likely candidate.

Just as she was thinking about him, the phone rang. Melanie knew it was Michael because nobody knew her number yet. She picked up the phone with a smile on her face. "Hey Michael .How did the car wash turn out?" Michael was surprised but pleased at her greeting. "Am I the only man who calls you Melanie? Is that how you knew it was me?" She didn't like the way he was thinking. Now this man is getting too sure of himself. "You are one of the few people that have my number, but I haven't had a chance to give it to all the other eligible men in town yet."

She could tell he was smiling, "You don't have to trouble yourself by giving it to anyone else. I'm the only man you need."

"Oh really now, you are a little sure of yourself Mr. Logan. I have told you over and over again that we are just friends."

"I know what you have said Melanie, but I also see in your eyes you feel more than friendship for me. I am waiting for the day when you finally admit it."

"Don't hold your breath. Michael, I can't talk about this right now. I have a lot on my mind and I can't handle anything else stealing my peace." She sounded upset. Michael realized he was going to have to stop pressuring her and be more patient. Knowing this to be true and doing it were two different things.

"What is bothering you Melanie, maybe I can help." He could really be annoying with this fixation he had about wanting to fix everything for her and rescue her from every situation. "There are some things you can't help me with, Michael" Even after she told him this she realized she needed to talk about it. Maybe God had worked this all out so that she would have someone to talk to. She took a deep breath and started talking.

"It has to do with my baggage I told you about. My father has gone to see Jerry and they have been talking about the past. Jerry wants me to see him. I was so hurt by him as a child that it would be very hard for me. I saw him once during the trouble with Jerry and he told me his sad tale. It was so different from what we heard from our mother all these years that I dismissed him without a second thought. Now I wonder if some of what he says is true. I just can't forget all the pain we all went through during that time. If I believe him, it means that I'd have to believe my mother lied to us for all those years."

She remembered the verse in Matthew 5:44 that says; *Love your enemies, do good to them which hate you, bless them that curse you, and pray for them that despitefully use you.*

Michael felt her strong emotions over the phone, "Honey, the truth may be somewhere in the middle. You know that when two people have the same experience together sometimes they see it in a totally different way. That's why witnesses to a crime sometimes have such different stories. I don't think you would have to believe your mother lied to you to give your father a chance to explain his side of the breakup."

Either his words made sense or she was reaching for any excuse to not feel like she would be betraying her dead mother by seeing her father. "I'll think about it" she sighed into the phone. "I've written my mother's sister, my Aunt Rose to see if she would give me some more information about that time. I was going to call but her number was out of order. I'm thinking she might have moved."

"Just pray and trust God Melanie. He will lead you to the truth. He told us that he is the way, the truth and the light." She thanked Michael for listening and hung up. She smiled when she remembered he never told her about the rest of the car wash and she never told him about the mishap at the shop.

He'll most likely call again just to talk about those details. Well talking on the phone is something friends do all the time. He is a good friend which something that she kept having to remind herself.

Chapter Ten

Melanie felt like she was expecting her own babies when she acquired a female Yorkshire terrier who was about to have a litter of puppies. Yorkies are such a cute and good-natured breed of dog. They are also small and intelligent and very desirable to a lot of people.

The puppies would be spoken for before they were weaned when people see how cute they were. The female was already showing signs of labor and Melanie was waiting with a lot of anticipation to see how many puppies she would have and if they would be born healthy. Melanie prepared a private area in the back of the shop for Flossie, the pregnant mother so she could have some privacy. She was keeping watch for any signs of distress and had a vet on standby in case of a problem. Seeing new life come into the world had always fascinated Melanie. It's such a miracle the way animals and people for that matter, reproduce themselves. What a testimony of how awesome God is. Just to think about the intricate details of each species of dog. Just to see the beauty of a kitten, or each tropical fish with the colors of the rainbow. Wow, this is the creator of us all and he is so good at the details.

Michael wanted to get a puppy for his niece Laura's birthday that was coming up. Melanie intended for him to have the pick of the litter. It would be a fortunate little puppy that went home with that little girl. She wanted a puppy so much that it sure wouldn't have a shortage of love. Krystal and David were the type of people who would certainly be responsible pet owners. Matching the right puppy with that family will be one of those rewarding times that make having a pet shop so much fun.

Flossie appeared to be doing well and it looked like the first puppy had made his appearance. It seemed to be pretty healthy as it wiggled closer to its mother. It looked like a boy and he was so cute and cuddly looking. Melanie resisted the urge to pick him up and examine him.

The others should come pretty quickly. Melanie checked on the dog but left her alone to deliver the other puppies. She believed there will be at least three judging from the size and shape of Flossie's belly. Small litters are more typical with small breeds.

The other animals needed to be fed and watered; the new shipment of supplies needed to be put away and the occasional customer had to be waited on. Melanie couldn't imagine having a job she could love any more. After the first few weeks in business, the pet shop seemed to be capable of earning her a decent living even with the added expense of Autumn's salary. Melanie was very content with her business, if only her personal life was doing as well.

She thought about the long awaited letter she received from her Aunt Rose yesterday. The letter confirmed her worst suspicions about her parents divorce. After the separation, their mother had taken them away so their father couldn't find them. Her mother had her entire family swear not to tell him where they were. Her father was telling them the truth about not knowing where they went. There had been a lot of arguments and intense fighting between her parents. Aunt Rose made it seem like there was fault on both sides. If she were to be biased it would be in favor of her baby sister so Melanie knew she was speaking the truth.

This changed everything she had always believed about her father. Even thinking the worst of him Melanie felt God had wanted her to forgive her father. She even went through a time when she thought she had forgiven him. Now that he was back in her life she knew she had been lying to herself. She still had a lot of hurt bottled up from spending her childhood believing her father had deserted her. The Bible tells us to examine ourselves and Melanie took a long hard look at her self and didn't like what she saw. Now, the question was what to do about it?

The first step was to ask forgiveness from the Lord. But the Bible is all too clear, if you have something against your brother that you should go to him and ask for forgiveness as well.

Melanie knew she had to talk to her father. The weight was hanging over her now and she had to do something to get rid of it. The big question was how that could happen when she had moved so far away. She decided to write to Jerry and see if she could get her father's phone number and address. She felt a little bit better after having made that decision. If God wanted her to reconcile with her father, he would have to help make a way. The Lord prayer says; *forgive us our debts as we forgive our debtors.* She wanted to remember God had forgiven her for her sins. Who was she to condemn her father?

Autumn came into the shop after School just in time to meet the three new arrivals. Flossie and her puppies were all doing fine. Melanie had everything all cleaned up and had transferred them into a new puppy habitat. The proud mother was the center of attention while Autumn told her what a good girl she was. She wanted to hold a puppy but Melanie told her it would be best if they waited a few days before they handled the new puppies. Just having the new puppies in the shop had them both so excited that it was hard to concentrate on getting any work done.

Melanie wanted to share the excitement with someone and on a whim decided to call Michael. It was time for him to be getting home from work just about now so she dialed his number. She had memorized it in case she needed his assistance again. He answered after the third ring.

"Hey Beautiful, how was your day? Melanie got flustered just from hearing his voice never mind the words he used. "How did you know it was me, or are you calling someone else beautiful?"

He laughed at her words, "I saw your number on caller I.D. Does this mean that if I was calling another woman beautiful, you would be jealous?" She wasn't sure how to get out of that question gracefully so she changed the subject. "I wanted to call and tell you about the new puppies I have at the shop. They are Yorkshire Terriers and I believe one of them would be perfect for Laura's birthday."

She began to tell him about the birth of the puppies and when they would be ready leave their mother. She chattered on and on about them and all that had been happening at the shop. She got so caught up in sharing it all with him she once again said more than she meant to. It just felt so good to have someone who seemed to care about what was important to her.

Michael in turn told her all about the progress on his building and how the work was stalled waiting for a shipment of specially made cornice for the front entrance. The brick masons couldn't finish the exterior until they had all the other pieces in place. It looked like he had a couple of free days on his hands. He planned to come by the shop and look at the new puppies in a day or two. They had no problem finding things to talk to one another about. The conversation flowed freely like they had known each other for years.

Michael thought about the phone call from Melanie after they had hung up. He felt such a strong connection with her. The way they shared their experiences with each other was exactly the way he had always imagined having a woman in his life would be. He had been praying for her and her situation with her father. He knew her lack of trust in him was rooted in her relationship with her father. He believed the Lord was going to help Melanie work through the pain of her parents divorce so she could be healed emotionally. The question he could not answer was how long this would take and if she would be ready for a relationship with him after it was settled.

If could be a mighty big word. This time it could be the difference between his happiness and his sorrow. Not having her in his life would be devastating for him. It was too late to protect his heart because he knew he already loved her and would love her until the day he died. She was the woman he had been praying for. The hard part for him was holding out hope that they would have a chance to be together.

It was Sunday morning and Melanie was spending some time talking to God before she got ready for church. She knew she couldn't put off a decision for much longer. The youth group needed to know if she was going to be able to be one of their leaders. She was undecided as she thought about the pros and cons of accepting this responsibility. Her time was often limited because of her pet shop but she had talked to Helen. She told her she would be willing to help out if she had an outing with the youth she needed to attend during shop hours. She would have to let them know up front that she might have to limit her activities to primarily when the shop was opened. She did feel a strong urge to work with the teens and she knew that if it was what God wanted her to do, he would make a way.

The verse that jumped out at her this morning during her devotions was Isaiah 50:4 that said; *The Lord God hath given me the tongue of the learned, that I should know how to speak a word in due season to him that is weary.* Being able to have a small part in helping those teenagers learn to live for the Lord would be worth a lot of sacrifice to her. If her brother would have had a strong Christian role model, his life might have been different. If one life could change direction it would be worth many hours of her time. Melanie knew she had to get her priorities straight. Was she more interested in her own goals or God's will? Was the fact that she would be thrown in even closer contact with Michael a reason to refuse? She can see it would be pretty selfish of her to refuse because of Michael or her shop. It looked like she would be accepting the position of youth leader. Now it was time for her to stop worrying and give it to God; if he hadn't been in control, her life would be a mess so she will trust him now. She felt a peace enter into her heart at this decision.

Monday turned out to be Melanie's first official outing with the teens. They had planned a clean up day and picnic on the beach. The kids had a teacher's workday and Michael was free at work and Melanie's shop is closed on Mondays so it all fell into place. The youth group had started picking up trash along the beach several years ago. It was a way for them to help the community to get the area ready for tourist season. As soon as the weather turned warm, the town would transform from a sleepy island community to a bustling tourist attraction. Preparation for the spring season had already started. The annual clean up day had become a tradition for the teens from church.

Melanie arrived at the designated meeting place late. Michael and five of the teenagers were waiting when she got there. She had been working on a picnic lunch. She loved to cook and found this a good opportunity to get creative with some take along foods. They quickly organized into groups of three and started to work. Cleanup day wasn't just about beautification of the town but also gave the teens a chance to get out and talk to the residents along the beach. This could provide an unexpected witnessing opportunity for them. A few new faces had shown up in church after one of these cleanup days. Seeing young people doing something unselfish for their community just seemed to make the seaside residents trust them more than they usually would. This group of kids had earned a good reputation in town.

Melanie loved the whole experience of cleanup day. Spending time getting to know the kids in the group and also meeting her new neighbors was worth the hard work. She had never been afraid to work. She believed she should lead by example. If the kids saw her shirking her part of the work, they would think it was okay for them to work half heartedly. Something about working together alongside one another seemed to build relationships.

She had already gotten to know Amber from the other week, and she found out a little bit more about her friend Penny. Penny was originally from Pennsylvania and had moved to the coast of North Carolina about three years ago with her parents. They owned a house directly on the beach. She had been having a hard time making friends before she got involved in church. She had a passion for serving God and wanted to go to Bible College and become a missionary. Penny was a remarkable girl and would be such a good influence on Autumn. Melanie couldn't help but think of how much Autumn could benefit from being a part of this group. She had invited her to come along today but Autumn had refused. Seeing the passion of youth on fire for serving God was an inspiration to Melanie.

They got a lot of work accomplished in the morning hours and had pre-arranged to meet back at the fishing pier to have lunch. So far Melanie had seen little of Michael and felt really good about her decision to be a leader for this group.

Melanie, Amber, and Penny came strolling up the beach with the picnic supplies in tow. They spread a couple of blankets right on the beach for everyone to sit down on for lunch. The three boys that were with Michael met them and started helping get the things from the car. As if by mutual consent, Michael stayed close to his group and Melanie to hers and they sat down to eat. Chad said a very heart-felt blessing and the food disappeared so quickly that Melanie thought the boys had inhaled theirs. Her special picnic food was a big hit.

The feeling of goodwill and fellowship seemed to be prevalent today as they shared the experiences of the morning. Michael and his group had met a new family in the area that seemed very interested in finding a home church. Somehow after all the hard work and food the kids still had energy left. They wanted to walk up to the pier and see if the fish were biting. Melanie said she would wait here and Michael told them to go ahead but to stay in sight. It seemed that all of the sudden the two of them were alone.

"I'm so glad you decided to help with the youth group Melanie. They seem to already be responding to you as their leader." He scooted over on the blanket closer to her propping himself up in a half sitting half laying position. Melanie turned on her side with her legs stretched out facing towards him.

"It wasn't a decision I made lightly Michael. I really sought God to be sure it was the right thing for me to do under the circumstances. I want us to agree that while we are with the kids we are on our best behavior. I don't want them to suspect anything is going on between us."

Michael turned toward her, "I don't want to upset you but they seem to already think we're a couple."

She frowned at him and showed her irritation; "What would make them think we are a couple?"

He brushed her hair back from her face, "It might have something to do with the fact that they have seen us sit together in church, and we have been to my mothers for dinner together and have even been seen around town together on occasion. This is a small town and we are part of a small church community. There is no reason to be ashamed. We are both single adults."

Melanie didn't like to think of herself as a source of gossip for any reason. She didn't think it would look good to the parents if the youth leaders were involved. She remembered how her old church asked her to step down from teaching because of the situation with her brother.

"Michael, what will their parents say? I don't want them to think we'd set a bad example for these kids." He wanted to hold her in his arms and reassure her but he knew it was not the time or place.

"Honey, we will not give them any reason to believe we are setting a bad example. It's not a sinful thing to date someone else as long as you don't cross the line. I care about you and I would never do anything to hurt your reputation. These people aren't going to be judge and jury to us just because we start to date. If anyone ever says anything to imply we are behaving in a way that would be a bad example to these kids, I will personally set them straight."

Melanie didn't believe it would be that simple but she didn't argue with Michael. She would like to think this new church would think the best of them but her experience was that people usually thought the worst of her. "Michael, I don't want to do anything that would hurt these kids. They are so on fire for God that if someone said something inappropriate about us it might turn them against the church." Michael thought about her words and realized it was a real possibility. "Then what we'll have to do is to get engaged."

Chapter Eleven

Melanie thought that Michael had flipped his wig. She reached over and playfully punched him in the arm. "Michael Logan we are not going to have to get engaged. That is ridiculous; this is not the eighteen hundreds you know."

He started laughing at her outraged expression and then he got completely serious as he lifted her head to look into his eyes. "Well the offer stands if you change your mind."

Looking at his face and seeing the expression in his eyes Melanie knew that if she went along with him they would be married before she knew what happened. She didn't know what to do with this guy. His behavior baffled her. She shook her head at his outrageous suggestion. "I'll keep that in mind." She knew she had some feelings for this man but entertaining the thought of marrying him was something that she would not allow herself to do. She still felt a strong need to protect herself. She would never tell him she hoped dealing with her past would help her to embrace a future. She couldn't consider what a future with him would mean to her. Even her daydreams could come back to haunt her later.

Michael knew he had shocked her. He had spoken his thoughts aloud without thinking about her reaction. He just seemed to loose his common sense when he was with her. It was his deepest wish for her to become his wife. He knew this woman was the helpmate God had created for him. Her past life had scarred her heart but he was praying for her healing. God was near to those with a broken heart.

He knew God has been working on Melanie's heart or she would not be considering her parents past relationship. The healing was getting ready to begin but her wounds would have to be reopened in order for her to put the past to rest. Michael prayed that the Lord would give her the strength to move forward. He knew if she gave up on the idea of learning about her father, it could mean the end of his chances to win her heart. He knew that if he could win her heart without reservation, it would be a treasure for him.

It had been two weeks since Melanie had written to her brother Jerry in jail to tell him about what Aunt Rose had said about their father. She had been awaiting a letter nervously ever since. So far the letter had not come. She had made up her mind to talk to her father and just wanted to know how Jerry felt about it. She didn't want to do anything to upset him. She was trying to decide how she would approach her father. She found out through Jerry that he had remarried but didn't have any more children. He said that he wanted to be a part of their lives. She wasn't sure what that would mean exactly.

The only way that he could be part of Jerry's life right now was to visit him in jail and to write. It could be a big change for her. He might want to get together on a regular basis. Now that she was starting to let go of the bitterness she had for her father she was starting to remember some happy times with him. She was awakened by a dream last night of her and Jerry following someone through the woods that was showing them different species of the plants they passed and pointing out how to identify animal tracks. When she woke up she realized it was actually a memory of her father. As Melanie started letting herself remember she knew that her love of animals had come from her father.

Her mother did not like any type of animal very much. She would complain about the cats in the house and the animals in the back yard. Another memory came to mind of fishing in a small boat with Jerry and her father. How could she have forgotten that he had taught her about nature? That was such an important part of who she had become. She wondered if she could open her heart to give him a chance to show her what type of man he really was. She had to let go of the ugly image of him that her mother had created.

She had to spend a lot of time taking her ugly thoughts captive as the bible says in 2 Corinthians 10:5 *Bringing into captivity every thought to the obedience of Christ.* She didn't realize how bitter her thoughts of her father had become. This had been an eye opening experience for her. She had felt comfortable in her Christianity when she moved to town. She thought of herself as a good Christian woman. How could a good Christian woman have such bitterness hidden inside her heart? She remembered the words of one of her favorite Psalms 130; *if thou Lord should mark iniquities, O Lord who shall stand? But there is forgiveness with thee.* Melanie thanked God for his forgiveness. She knew that if she wanted to be a good Christian example she would have to give that same forgiveness to her father.

Felix the monkey had become quite the clown. He had figured out he could get out of his habitat if he did tricks for the people who came to the shop. He and Pepe' had people very entertained with their show stopping trick which had Felix riding on the small dogs back like a cowboy. Pepe' liked to come to work with Melanie so he could do his tricks with Felix. They both loved all the attention they got from the customers. The only time he didn't want to leave home was if Peaches was outside. If he saw Peaches he would immediately go to his side of the fence and start to whine. It was a pitiful sound and it was one of the reasons Melanie had started bringing him to the shop with her. He really needed to get a grip.

As she predicted, the monkey being part of the shop was a good way to bring in business. She had even thought about keeping him as a permanent part of "God's Little Creatures". The shop was doing better than she had expected. When the word got around town about the monkey, animal lovers had started coming in to see him. While the animal lovers were in the shop they usually purchased something. Melanie made a point to find out if there was anything they needed that wasn't on the shelves. She would try to have the requested items in stock the next time the customers came in. This personal service was something people appreciated. This was bringing people back again and again. The future of the shop was looking secure. When tourist season hit she expected the business to pick up even more.

Melanie had decided she could afford another part time clerk. She was planning to hire a high School aged boy so they would have some one to help with the large bags of various animal foods. If one of the boys in the youth group needed a summer job, she would like to hire them before she considered anyone else. Having a Christian boy around the shop would be good for Autumn. She had not seen many positive male role models in her life. Melanie knew from personal experience that not having a positive male role model can really make your view of men twisted.

Autumn seemed to be changing daily. She had taken out some of her strange jewelry and had stopped painting her nails black. She had also started wearing more normal teenage clothes. Melanie could see that the girl wanted to fit in here. They had several long conversations about being an individual inside and becoming what God had created you to be. Melanie had never openly criticized the way she looked. She had tried to show her she found her valuable just the way she was. This seemed to be giving her more confidence.

All the criticism from her Aunt had made her want to act more rebellious. Melanie had prayed about how to deal with Autumn and had come to realize that unconditional acceptance and love was what everyone really wants. That is what we get from a strong relationship with the Lord. Autumn had never felt accepted and loved for herself. Her mother had found her to be an inconvenience and her Aunt seemed to find her a difficult trial. Autumn was starved for love and acceptance. Melanie knew that this girl coming into her shop had been no accident. God was at work in her life and Melanie was just amazed she was being given the opportunity to be a part of it. She felt so blessed.

Autumn was working at the front of the shop and Melanie was back with the puppies when Michael came in. Melanie had not seen him for a few days. He looked especially handsome today in his typical khaki pants and sport shirt. The color of the shirt brought out his eyes. She caught his arrogant look when he saw her sizing him up and frowned at him.

"Hey Melanie, why the long face?" She knew he was being amused at her expense and she decided to turn the tables on him. "I was just watching you come in just now. I wondered why such a handsome guy was wasting his time hanging around with his good buddy instead of getting out there and finding himself a woman." She grinned at him and went back to filling the puppy's water dish.

He didn't say anything for a few minutes. He just watched her with an intense look on his face. "Well my good buddy Melanie, how about you show me those puppies you are so fond of." She was almost disappointed that he didn't seem to want to trade quips with her.

She showed him into the puppy habitat and picked up one of the puppies. "Are these little guys the cutest things you ever saw?" He took the puppy and examined it carefully "This little pup is going to steal a certain little girl's heart as soon as she sees him." He could say he knew the feeling because Melanie had done that very thing to him.

Michael and Melanie looked over all the puppies and he decided on a sweet little female who seemed to like to be held and petted. Melanie told him she would save the pup for him and as they were walking toward the door of the puppy habitat, they bumped into one another. Melanie jumped back like she had been burned. Michael found this fact amusing because he knew she felt the same connection that he did when they touched. He was encouraged by this bit of information and tucked it back in his mind to examine later. He figured he might as well take a chance so he decided to ask her to dinner. He motioned toward the door and put his hand on her back as he led her out. He followed close behind.

"So what have you got to do after work this evening?" He would get her to admit to not having plans before he presented his.

Melanie was waking toward the front of the store not really paying attention to his casual question, "Not much just dinner with the boys and a good book."

"How about we hop into that little car of yours and put the top down and go for a drive up to Wilmington?" Since it was a very warm day for late winter, he knew she would enjoy a ride with the top down. While she was thinking about it, he continued to make his case. "I'm just your good buddy Mike and I want to go out for Italian. There's a great little restaurant that you'll love and we can be there in forty five minutes. Autumn can close up the store for you and we can get on the road right now, what do you think?"

Melanie loved to do things on the spur of the moment. Michael was getting to know her too well. He was making her an offer she found hard to refuse. "Well I think I'd love to have dinner with my good buddy Mike but it's just a dinner between friends, not a date."

Michael didn't care what they called it as long as he was spending the evening with this special woman he was a happy man. "Sounds like a plan. How soon can you be ready to leave?"

She looked around the shop and thought about what had to be done. "Give me ten minutes and I'll meet you by the car."

The drive turned out to be a side splitting funny time together. Melanie put on some music and started to sing. Saying she was not blessed with a nice singing voice would be an understatement. It was very off key and all over the place. In short it was just plain horrible. Michael wasn't ready for the choir either but he could carry a tune in a bucket for about a quarter of a mile. That was the comment that he got from Melanie on his singing.

When she started on the first song, he was trying hard not to laugh or cover his ears. He didn't know if she knew how bad she was. When she got louder, they passed a barking dog and she grinned at him. He just grinned back and decided to sing along. When she heard his rough baritone voice that sounded a lot like he had a frog down in his throat, she couldn't help herself, she started to laugh. When she started laughing, so did he and they were doubling over in laughter at each other.

"I hope you don't think that you're any better than I am honey because you could make the paint on the barn curl up with your singing voice." She laughed back at him, "Well you could give the alley cats in the neighborhood the confidence to start a symphony."

They traded insults for a while and then they decided to crank it up and sing anyway. It was the kind of companionship you would share with a good buddy but there was always that little zing of electricity between them to keep them on their toes. They sang all the way into town until they decided they didn't want to get a ticket for disturbing the peace.

When they got to the restaurant, they were relaxed and happy. Michael found out something he didn't know about Melanie. She was never going to be boring. She could make a simple dinner in the city fun. They talked freely with each other but as if by prior mutual agreement stayed away from any heavy subjects.

The food was wonderful and they enjoyed the meal so much Melanie wanted to compliment the chef. Michael told her that the people in North Carolina don't compliment the chef. He was probably some pimple faced kid the owner had taught a few recipes. She insisted on at least leaving him a note so she wrote a little note on her napkin and asked the waiter to give it to the chef. Michael busted out laughing when the young waiter said, "That's not the chef, that's my cousin John."

On the ride home, they looked at the stars for a while and then Melanie got cold so they put the top up. She had enjoyed this evening with Michael a lot. She was beginning to relax and be herself more around him and she was happy with the result. He was a lot of fun. Melanie had a firm belief that Christians as a whole needed to loosen up and have more fun. The joy of the Lord is a gift. She and Michael had more in common than bad singing voices. She was seeing that what he keeps telling her could be the truth. They could be happy together as a couple.

As she chewed on that thought for a while he turned toward her in the driver's seat and said, "A penny for your thoughts." There was no way she was going to feed his oversized ego by telling him she was thinking about him.

"I was just thinking about all I have to do tomorrow." This wasn't exactly a lie because she had thought about it earlier.

He reached over and picked up her hand. "I was thinking about what a good buddy you are." He raised his eyebrows and grinned at her and she pulled her hand from his grip and swatted him on the shoulder. She turned her eyes ahead and told him one small truth.

"You have been a wonderful friend to me since we met, Michael. I want to thank you for that."

He looked at her as if he didn't like that comment. "I won't tell you again what I think of all this good friend business of yours Melanie. Let's just enjoy the rest of this evening together. We'll be back to town soon."

They enjoyed the silence of the night and the companionship for the rest of the drive home. Melanie pulled into the pet shop parking lot where he had left his truck. He got out of her car and went around to her side of the car to tell her goodnight. Melanie felt a sudden sadness that the night had to end. He had eased her loneliness for a while and helped her to relax and have a little fun. So she got out of the car and walked toward him and grabbed his arm. As he turned around she went into his arms. "Can I have a hug before you go?"

He was only too happy to comply with her request. As she pulled herself from his arms, she got into her car and drove away and left him standing there with a bemused expression on his face. This woman was going to drive him crazy. All night she stressed the fact several times they were just friends but couldn't leave him without a hug. He couldn't figure her out but he sure did like trying. He had a hopeful, happy heart as he drove home.

Melanie arrived home to find her cats waiting at the door. Lance acted insulted that she had left them so long. Newman was just glad to see her. Pepe' was spending the night at the shop since he had come to work with her this morning. Melanie was feeling joyful and worried at the same time. The more time she spent with Michael the more she was coming to care for him. She had started enjoying his protective ways and his big ego. That couldn't be a good sign. How could she take a chance on being rejected by him? She had this fear that even if she eventually ended up getting married to him, she might still come home and find him gone one day.

When had she started considering even the remotest possibility of marrying him anyway? It had to be when he made that outrageous suggestion at the beach. She felt like crying because she didn't know if she could ever give anyone, even Michael, the power to hurt her that way. She knew it wasn't a normal reaction to having a wonderful man who wanted a relationship with her, but she was not a normal woman. She didn't know if she ever would be.

Chapter Twelve

Melanie woke up after spending the biggest part of her night on her knees and in tears. She was wrestling with herself about her future. She had made a decision. She would tell Michael they could start dating. She knew what she really wanted was a future with him and the possibility of marriage and children. It was really the desire of her heart that she has been afraid to voice out loud.

She was going to contact her father also. Fear is the opposite of faith and it was not going to rule her life anymore. Today was going to be the first day of the rest of her life. She is going to remember that the Bible says in Philippians 4:13, *I can do all things through Christ who strengthens me.* Now the next step was to come up with a plan to ask Michael out on a real date. But right now she has to get ready to go to work.

Helen was coming to the shop today. She was going to spend some time there learning how to handle things for Melanie in case she needed to be out of the store for an occasional day. Autumn could be a great help but she had to go to School and Melanie needed to have someone else she could call on, just in case. Helen had surprised Melanie by offering to be her backup person. Melanie knew it was not for money because Helen didn't need more income. She told Melanie she wanted the opportunity to get to know people in the community. She had friends from her church but she had always been a subject of gossip to the townspeople. She seemed to be excited at the prospect of helping out in the shop. She was an animal lover and a people person. Her outrageous hats would add a little color to the shop. As long as people were talking about the cute little monkey or the funny hat lady, they were keeping an interest in coming in to buy things. It was like free publicity for them.

Helen showed up just in time to help Melanie feed, water and clean up after the animals. This was the part of the job Melanie was afraid might be offensive to Helen. It could be unpleasant to clean up the messes the animals made. Helen didn't seem to mind at all. She told Melanie she had been a mother after all and had experienced changing diapers so this was a breeze. Helen wore her hat with the small animal on top today. It was the first hat that Melanie had seen her wear. It seemed somehow appropriate for the shop.

As Melanie went to let Felix out of his cage, he did an uncharacteristic thing. He jumped right over to Helen's shoulder. He hadn't shown any interest in being so friendly with anyone else except Melanie. He startled Helen at first but then she was laughing at his antics. He had taken a liking to her hat so he pulled it from her head and starting chattering to it and then tried to put it on his own head. It was way too large and he chattered at it when his eyes got covered. It was amazing how well they took to one another.

Helen seemed to love the little guy and didn't mind having him perched on her shoulder at all. Just as they were getting him settled down, Pepe' came over and started barking at him. It was like they could communicate with each other each in their own language. Felix jumped from Helen's shoulder and down to greet his friend.

Then the small dog and the monkey started playing together. The monkey chattered away at the dog and the dog seemed to enjoy the conversation. They went over to the dog toy section and found a ball Melanie let them play with. Helen was delighted by the entire scene and Melanie saw she was a natural in the shop and now she would have a dependable back up to work in the shop that she could count on.

A delivery van pulled into the construction site where Michael was working and Michael wondered what they could be delivering. He wasn't expecting any building supplies that would be delivered by a van. They must be in the wrong place. He sent one of his men out to help direct them since they must be lost. To his surprise the man that he sent came back in with a big smile on his face. "It's a delivery for you, Mike. Maybe you'd better go see for yourself."

Michael was annoyed that he had to waste his time with this nonsense. He was on a schedule and had plenty of work to keep him busy. He walked out to the van preparing to explain that there had been a mix up. Then he read the name on the side of the van and was puzzled. It said "Florist." Michael's face turned a bright shade of red when the young man handed him some roses with a balloon attached. The balloon said, "Be mine" obviously a leftover from Valentines Day. The roses were red. He shook his head because he still couldn't believe this was happening until he read the note.

Roses are red Violets are blue
I would like to go out with you
Not as a friend or a trusty first mate
How about going on a real date?
If you're still willing
I'll pick you up at eight.

Yours,
Melanie

He couldn't help himself. He started laughing. The men on the construction site were looking at him like he'd lost his mind. He hadn't lost his mind yet but he had lost his heart to a brown-eyed, curly-haired, crazy angel. She was making his head go around in circles with her antics but what fun it is along the way. He started walking toward his truck to put the flowers in the front seat. He looked back over his shoulder and told his superintendent he'd be back later. He wasn't going to wait until eight to see her. She didn't know how happy she had made him today but he was going to go over to the shop and tell her. His patience was beginning to pay off. She

111

was asking him out on a date. She really was full of surprises. He loved surprises and he knew she liked them too. She was going to get a surprise in about ten minutes.

Melanie was at the front register when Michael came into the shop. Helen had gone home earlier and Autumn wasn't scheduled to come in for a couple of hours yet. When she saw him she suddenly felt shy and unsure of herself. He didn't say anything right away because she was helping a customer. He just stood over to the left of the counter and pretended to be looking at some rawhide chews. When he caught her looking at him from the corner of her eye he winked.

She turned away and pretended she didn't see. It took about five minutes for her to finish showing the man the various types of flea spray. As soon as he left the store, they were alone together and Melanie was feeling a little nervous.

"Hey Michael, what brings you by this afternoon? There was always the possibility he hadn't got the flowers yet. He didn't answer her right away, just started motioning for her to come closer by crooking his index finger. She stepped a little closer. "Did you get the flowers?"

He nodded his head in the positive and kept motioning her closer. When she was standing about three feet away she stopped. "Your making me nervous Michael, was there something that you wanted to tell me?" He took a step closer to her and put his hands on her shoulders. He looked into her eyes and she saw something in his that was intense and a little frightening to her.

"It seems that someone I know has sent a message proclaiming to all within a half a mile of my job that she wanted me to be hers. I am all too happy to accommodate that request." He pulled her into his arms and held her against his chest. "I have been yours from the first minute I laid eyes on you little lady, now what do you purpose to do with me?"

She pulled away and looked at his face, "I'd thought I'd take you on a real date tonight and see how you act." She grinned up at him and gave a sigh of relief at the twinkle on his eyes.

He looked solemnly into her eyes and was quiet for a minute. "And just what would be the difference between a real date and the dinners we've already had together just so I understand the rules."

She pulled away from him again and looked down at her shoes, "Well I guess it would mean I would be willing to consider being your woman and not just your friend. That would mean we would be a couple and spend time getting to know each other better."

He put his fist under his chin in a thinking position like he was considering what she had said. "I believe I would like for you to be my woman, does that mean that I'd be your man?" She realized he was teasing her but she couldn't pretend that this wasn't serious to her.

"I'd like to think we might have a relationship with one another but I can't tell you I'm over my concerns and fears because that wouldn't be true. I have decided that I don't want to let fear rob me of my chance at happiness with you. You're a fine man and any woman would be proud to call you hers." She smiled up at him with her heart in her eyes.

He pulled her close to his heart again not believing how blessed he felt right now. "Melanie you have made me a happy man. There is one more thing I need to ask you before I leave and let you get back to work. "Could I kiss you?"

She looked up at him and shyly nodded her head yes. He pulled her gently towards him and kissed her gently and reverently. She didn't even think of slugging him. She closed her eyes and felt the magic of the moment. This was her first real kiss because the incident years ago in the barn didn't really count and the little peck he gave her in the shop wasn't a real kiss either. She surprised herself by liking it.

He let her go and just looked at her for a few seconds, and then he turned to go. "I'll be ready at eight." and he went back out the door.

Well she'd done it now Melanie thought. She hoped she could deal with the consequences. Michael was a very good man but he still frightened her a little. She saw that he wanted a serious relationship with her. He had made her think that he might care for her already.

She has made a really big step today but she wanted to take some baby steps from now on. The trouble was that Michael Logan had really big feet.

Melanie decided she would wear a nice dress and pumps tonight. She took her hair down and put on some makeup too. She really wanted tonight to be special. The first real date she had planned for them wouldn't be what he was expecting. She had planned a moonlight picnic on the beach with soft music and candles to set the romantic mood. She was really trusting Michael to be a gentleman because they would be alone. She thought they could dance on the beach and maybe take a walk along the shore. If they got bored with that she had the supplies for making smores. The marshmallow, chocolate cookie treats were one of her favorites. There was a barbeque pit near by and she had gotten permission for them to use it. She had everything she thought they would need.

Melanie pulled into Michael's drive way at eight o'clock sharp. He was waiting on his front porch for her. She got out and walked over to meet him. He looked especially handsome tonight with some nice jeans and a dress shirt topped with a sports jacket. The jacket emphasized his broad shoulders and arms. Sometimes Melanie forgot how big he was. He was a gentle giant though and she wasn't really afraid he'd ever hurt her physically. It was the power of the emotions he invoked in her that let her know she could be hurt emotionally by this man.

"Hey Michael, are you ready to go?" He grabbed her hand and walked with her back to the car.

"Just where are we going Miss Melanie? You are going to have to share that little piece of information with me."

She just swung their arms back and forth as they walked and giggled. "It's going to be fine dining with the best view in town."

He went around and opened her door on the driver's side of Old Yeller and then went around and got in. She started the car and put it into gear.

"You know if you don't mind, I'd like to drive next time. I'm a little big for this little yellow car of yours." He tried to adjust his legs into a more comfortable position.

She looked over at him as she pulled into the street, "I don't mind but you could clean the old truck up a little bit first." He looked over for his reaction. He was smiling.

"I can't believe this, you've only been my woman one day and your already trying to give me orders. I can take a hint Miss Melanie; I'll clean the truck up first I promise. I usually don't have pretty ladies riding around in it with me."

She frowned back at him, "I'm not your woman yet Mr. Logan, and I'm just giving you a trial run to see if you know how to treat a lady."

"I'll keep that in mind," he said as he began to pay attention to the direction she was driving.

"Just where is this fine dining with a great view?" He knew all the restaurants in town and there wasn't anything in this direction. She decided to break the suspense, "We are going to have a romantic picnic on the beach."

He was pleased with this turn of events. "That sounds like a wonderful idea to me."

She pulled into the parking area and pulled up the park break. "Just remember I trust you to be a gentleman." He looked offended at her words. "Melanie I've told you honey I would never do anything to hurt you or your reputation."

She put her hand on the door handle to get out, "I do trust you or we wouldn't be here."

They got the blanket and hamper out of the car and started walking out to find a nice spot on the beach. She had brought a flashlight to help them get settled before they lit the candles, but they really didn't need it. The moon was out and there was enough light to walk by. They found a nice spot and spread out the blankets and sat down. Melanie started pulling out the candles and other items as Michael looked out over the ocean. "This is a really nice idea. I'm glad you thought of it." She lit the candles and settled back beside him. "I love the ocean, that's why I moved so far away from home to be close to it."

He was silently looking out at the ocean. "If it brought you to me, then I love the ocean too. It's becoming my favorite place."

They had a quiet dinner together that was so different from their last night with the laughter. The electricity between them was stronger now that they had made this step into romance. They talked to each other about their hopes and dreams. They talked to each other about their likes and dislikes. Then they talked to each other about non-consequential things. It was a nice evening just getting to know each other as she had planed. Melanie knew they should go home soon but she hated for the evening to end. She looked over at him and picked up his large hand.

"How would you feel about a walk down the beach?" They rose together with their hands joined as they went strolling in the direction of the pier. She had removed her shoes because of the sand and after they had gone a little ways felt a sharp sting on her foot. She stumbled and he kept her from falling. "I think I stepped on something sharp."

She held her food up to the flashlight and there was an ugly gash that was bleeding generously. When he saw it he looked a little worried, "Here I'll carry you back to the car. It looks like you'll need some stitches in this foot." He picked her up like she weighed almost nothing and carried her. She didn't think it was necessary to be carried but she liked it. "Get me over to the streetlight so I can see how bad it is. I don't want to bleed on my good dress." It looked like it would need a stitch or two and she told him to get their things and she'd go to the hospital.

He put her down near the light as he ran back and gathered up their things. He made record time as he came back and deposited her into the passenger seat. "Let me have the keys." He reached over the seat for them. She held them in her hand another minute and tried to reason with him. "There's no reason you have to go with me. I'll just wrap it up and drive into Southport."

He snatched the keys from her hand, "I will not argue with you Melanie, I'm taking you to the hospital." He was so stern in his pronouncement that she didn't say anything further. Sometime a take charge man was a good thing.

Chapter Thirteen

The drive to Southport was nerve racking for Melanie because Michael had decided to go back into his hero fixation again and was driving way too fast. He must have thought Melanie was going to bleed to death from a cut on the foot. He really needed to calm down. Melanie was secretly amused at his high handed behavior. He was taking charge in this mini crisis like a general marching into battle. She wondered how he'd be in a real life and death crisis. When he saw the blood pouring out of her foot, he looked like he might faint for a minute. His face got a little white before he took a deep breath and swept her up into his arms. She rather liked that part of this little mishap. Being carried like she was a fragile doll that might break was a new experience for her. She wanted to see if she could get him to lighten up and spoke her thoughts out loud. Maybe a little flirting would help.

"Hey handsome, if you are this intense over a cut foot how would you be it something serious would happen? It's just a few stitches no big deal. I'll be fine in just a little while. I did like the way you carried me to the car though." She reached over and touched his arm as he drove. "Thank you for taking such good care of me."

He reached over and touched her face gently, "You liked that huh? I kind of liked holding you in my arms but I can't stand the thought of your being hurt. I'd be willing to practice carrying you in my arms some more later, if you feel like it." He looked over at her and winked. "Are you in pain, honey?" His face showed genuine concern.

I'm just fine; the bleeding has slowed down a lot since we wrapped it up. It doesn't hurt too much. I'm just wondering how I'll handle the store tomorrow."

"Didn't you tell me tonight that Helen was going to help you in the store when you needed her?"

"That's true but she has only had a little training with me today to learn the ropes. I hate to ask her to handle it all alone especially on such short notice." Michael tried to persuade her to reconsider. "I know she'll be willing to help out. She can call you about anything that comes up. You should rest tomorrow and stay off that foot." She thought he was getting a little bossy. She had to make him understand her store was a priority to her.

"Don't think for one minute you are going to tell me what to do, especially when it comes to the store? My store is very important to me. I've worked long and hard to get it and I'll do what I have to, in order to keep it open."

He chuckled at her intensity, "Calm down Miss Melanie, your store will still be there if you stay home for one day and rest your foot. I hear you loud and clear. You are an independent business woman and you make your own decisions. I just want you to take care of yourself and you might as well know that I plan to be the one making sure that you do."

She didn't comment because they were pulling in to the emergency room entrance. He got out of the car and went around and tried to pick her up to carry her in. She insisted on walking on her own with him supporting her as she hopped in the hospital. She had no intention of being carried into the hospital like an invalid. He reluctantly agreed but held her side so the majority of her weight was supported by him. As they went into the doors of the hospital he rushed up to the desk. "We need to see a doctor right away."

Melanie sat down with the required paperwork and waited patiently. Michael was not however a patient man. "How long before she sees a doctor? Can't you see she's bleeding all over the place?"

The nurse reassured him that she would be seen as soon as possible and Michael reluctantly sat back down beside her. He might not have even been aware of it but he put his arm around the back of her chair and rubbed her arm as if to sooth her. She found she was really getting to know a lot more than she expected to about Michael tonight. The more she saw of him, the more she appreciated what a strong capable man he was. She also saw he seemed to be genuine in his feelings for her. The future with this man in it might not be too bad. He just had to learn not to be so bossy.

On the drive home from the hospital, Melanie leaned her head over and went to sleep. They had given her something for pain and it must have made her drowsy. She had finally agreed to call Helen and see if she could open the store for her tomorrow. Helen was only too glad to help out. The doctor had recommended she stay off her foot for a couple of days. Michael intended to see that she followed doctor's orders. The hard part would be overcoming her stubborn streak. He felt he was up to the challenge.

She woke up as they pulled into her driveway. She got her keys and started to get out of the car. Michael was waiting for her and scoped her up in his arms. She didn't mind too much because she was very sleepy. He unlocked the door to the house and brought her in, placing her gently on the couch. He wanted to see her settled before he called a friend to come over and pick him up. Since he had ridden with her this evening, he was temporarily stranded here at her house. He knew she would have a fit if he mentioned staying to look after her but that was exactly what he wanted to do.

What was it about this woman that made him feel like he should protect her from harm? He had never felt the need to protect anyone else like this. It was a powerful emotion that came over him when he saw she was hurt. He didn't know what he would do if something would happen to her. It was something he couldn't even think about right now and maybe never. She might not have made a commitment to him yet, but he knew from the center of his being that he was committed to this woman for life. If she didn't marry him he'd never marry anyone else. He hoped and prayed that she would develop feelings for him. It was really in God's hands. It was just hard for Michael to let go and trust him. Michael placed a glass of water and her pain medication on the table by the couch. He covered her with an afghan and just watched her sleep until his friend showed up.

The morning came and Melanie didn't remember coming home. She remembered getting a shot at the hospital and taking some pain pills for the ride home. Her foot really hurt but she wasn't about to admit it to Michael. She smiled as she thought of him. Last night had been a magical evening before her accident. The moonlight dinner had been a success. They hadn't talked about going out on another date but she knew she'd see him soon. It was still pretty early in the morning so she decided to hop into her room and sleep for a while longer. She joined her cats in the bed and quickly fell back to sleep.

She awoke to a loud knocking at her door. She hobbled over to see who it was and found none other than the man she had been dreaming about. She looked out and saw him and groaned. She hadn't had a shower or even brushed her teeth. He needed to come back later. "Go away, I'm sleeping." She spoke to the back of the door.

"Open the door Miss Melanie, I brought you some breakfast." She was a little hungry but she still didn't want to let him in.

"What did you bring?" Her curiosity was rearing its ugly head.

"I brought you some coffee and juice and eggs with bacon and grits." She could hear the smile in his voice.

"Did you get up and cook for me this morning?" She was really curious now.

"Nope, it's a plate of breakfast from the diner. They have the best breakfast in town."

She opened the door and let him in. "I'm not ready for company yet but I'll take the food."

He came in and set the bags on the table. "I wanted to make sure you were alright here by yourself this morning." He turned around and looked her over to see for himself that she was fine.

"I told you I wasn't ready for company. It's not nice to stare at a person who's not at her best." She sounded a little grumpy.

"You look beautiful in the morning, honey; you don't have to worry about fixing yourself up for me." He turned to go and gave her a quick kiss on the cheek as he passed by. "I'll call you later."

As she stood at the door and watched him get into his truck he said, "I washed the old truck this morning first thing. I wouldn't want my woman to have to ride in a dirty truck." She smiled and pointed her finger in his direction. "I'm not your woman yet; don't get too sure of yourself."

She took a shower and called Helen to go over some final things she wanted to tell her about the store. She had a whole day of rest ahead of her and she wanted to start by spending some time reading her Bible. She always felt like she had to rush through her devotional time in the mornings. Today she had as much time as she wanted. She was going to enjoy it.

About eleven thirty she heard a knock on her door. She was not surprised this time to find Michael with lunch. He came in and crowded close to her as she stood holding the door open for him because his hands were full. He brushed a quick kiss on her cheek. "Honey I'm home," he said with a big smile. She swatted at him as he passed by. "Behave yourself I'm an injured woman." He sat the bags on the table and started pulling out what looked like sub sandwiches and potato chips.

"I'd thought I'd stay a while and have lunch with you if you don't mind." He glanced her way with a skeptical look in his eye.

"Well since your feeding me I guess you can stay. I've had my coffee and shower so I'm ready for a little company." She sat down at the table and let him serve her.

"I hope you like roast beef and potato salad. I got some chips and slaw too just in case." He placed the food in front of them and sat down. He looked at her and nodded and as if they had been doing it this way for years, they bowed their heads together to say a blessing.

He stayed for about an hour and a half and then went back to work. Melanie called the shop to see how Helen was doing and was surprised and a little disappointed that she was doing very well. The sales had been steady. She had taken care of the animals needs and she was enjoying the whole experience more than she thought she would. She was insisting on opening the shop tomorrow for Melanie as well since it was Saturday and she would have until Monday to rest her foot. Melanie hated to agree but she knew it would be hard for her to work until her foot was a little better. It looked like she had a whole weekend ahead to rest and relax. It was hard for her to rest and relax because she was accustomed to being busy.

Melanie went out to get the mail and found the letter she had been waiting for from her brother Jerry. She was hoping to hear from him but now that she held the letter in her hand she hesitated to open it. She took a deep breath, said a little prayer and tore the envelope open.

Dear Mel,

I was hurt and surprised when I got your letter. I never would have dreamed that Momma lied to us all those years. It's hard to imagine how different our life would have been if we had been able to know our father. I don't really remember him living with us at all. I am angry at Momma for doing this and it makes me feel ashamed of myself to be angry at a dead woman. I wish I could talk to her and find out why this happened. She must have thought that she was doing the right thing by keeping us apart from him. I don't know how I feel.

The old man came to see me again and I talked to him about you. I think we should give him a chance. I hope you won't be mad at me but I gave him your address and phone number. He knows that you talked to Aunt Rose about him too.

I wasn't trying to make you do anything you didn't want to do, but he wants to talk to you. He kept talking about his little girl who used to follow along behind him through the woods. He told me he used to take us on hikes when we were small and try to teach us about plants and animals. I don't remember anything about it but I know that you used to do that with me when I was little. Do you remember him as our daddy?

Rachel has not contacted me again and I wish I knew how she's doing. I would feel so much better if I knew for sure she was still clean from the drugs. So you think that you could make a call or two and find out for me. I know how you feel about her but it keeps me up at night wondering.

I love you girl and don't you ever forget it. Write me and let me know what's going on in your new life. I want to know if you talk to the old man too.

Love,
Jerry

Melanie put the letter down and thought about her father. She did have a memory of him. He had been patient and kind to her as a child. It was comforting to know this small piece of information. The thing she thought about and couldn't seem to get past is that her mother who was the one person that she would have thought would never betray her really had.

How was she supposed to trust people when her own family was so messed up? Tears ran down her face as she thought of her mother and the words she had spoken to them when they asked about their father. It was a cruel thing to do to children.

"Lord, please help me to forgive her. Lord, please help me to forgive him." She knew it didn't make sense but she still had bad feelings and anger towards him. He should have fought harder for them. He should have looked longer. He shouldn't have given up on his children. Parents should never give up on their children. She gave in to her sobs and cried herself back to sleep.

Michael came in and found her a short time later asleep on the couch with dried tears on her face. He had knocked but she must not have heard him so he tried the door and it was unlocked. He touched her on the shoulder gently to awaken her. "Honey, what's wrong? Is your foot hurting you this much?" He had sat down on the edge of the couch.

When she woke up and saw him there she was still a little disoriented from sleep and her emotions. She wrapped her arms around him and just held him close to her heart. She didn't want to talk about her pain right now; she just wanted to feel comfort. He held her gently in his arms and wondered what in the world had her so upset. He could tell she was upset and hurting from her actions.

She pulled away from him and tried to get herself together. "I just got a letter from Jerry and it upset me. I don't really want to talk about it right now." He didn't say a word, just picked up her hand and held it softly. He knew he had come in on her at a bad time but wasn't sorry. She needed him and he would be there for her no matter what.

He spent the evening at her house trying to cheer her up. They cooked hot dogs on her tiny little grill in the backyard. He tried to impress her with his cooking skills, limited as they were. They watched an old movie on television and sat on the couch together with the two cats and dog trying to snuggle in between them. It was a nice evening just being together and hanging out. They popped popcorn and threw it at each other. Then they cleaned up the mess. The companionship they shared with each other came naturally and Michael knew how rare a gift that was.

When it started to get late, he knew it was time to go home because she was looking a little worn out. "Melanie, I'm going to go before my stimulating company puts you to sleep." She stood up to walk him to the door.

"Thanks for feeding me today and for spending the evening here keeping me company when you could have been doing something more interesting." He turned and faced her.

"There's no place I'd rather be than here with you." Her faced turned a little red but she didn't really believe him.

"I'm not sure I believe that, it sound like a line to me." She grinned at him.

He just shook his head at her nonsense. "I don't have any lines to say to women. I've spent the last few years trying to get away from them until I met you." She put her arms around him and reached up and kissed him sweetly.

"Good night Michael. I've heard enough sweet talk for one night." He touched her face reverently and turned to go. "I'll call you tomorrow and we can discuss some plans for our next date. Don't try to walk to the door I'll let myself out. Good night Melanie."

Chapter Fourteen

Melanie was at home resting her foot on Saturday when she heard a knock at her door. She figured it would be Michael even though he told her he had to go to the construction site this morning. He had been keeping close tabs on her since she cut her foot. She was feeling thankful that God had brought him into her life. She had a nice quiet time this morning and was feeling so peaceful about her life. She knew that she had been blessed and didn't want to forget to be thankful.

She hobbled over to the door and opened it without looking to see who was there. When she saw her father standing on her doorstep she froze. He lived in Richmond. What was he doing here? She wanted to close the door in his face but she didn't give in to her urge.

"Won't you come in?" She let him into the house and they sat down in the living room. He was on the couch and she was on the chair opposite him. They were both silent for a couple of minutes before he spoke. "What happened to your foot?" He inclined his head toward her bandage.

"It's just a few stitches, nothing major. I'll be fine in a few days." She took a deep breath. "What are you doing here? I didn't invite you to come." She didn't mean to sound so harsh but this was not a pleasant surprise. She found herself completely unprepared to talk with this man. He was a stranger to her.

"I had to come and see you Melanie. I have wanted to see you and spend time with you for so long and when Jerry gave me your address, I couldn't seem to stop myself from driving out here to see you."

Lancelot jumped up on her lap and she felt comfort in having him near her. "He gave you my address so you could write to me not come out here." She couldn't help but have some negative emotions that were evident in her voice.

"I thought if we could just talk face to face, I could explain what happened all those years ago. I never meant to leave you and Jerry. Your mother and I had a bad marriage but I always loved the two of you. She did the most hurtful thing she could do by keeping you away from me."

She held her hand up in protest. "I will not tolerate your bad mouthing my mother. She can't defend herself and I have only heard your side of why she moved us away. She must have had a good reason."

He looked visibly upset as he tried to reason with her. "I am sorry for the pain you have suffered because of your mother and I and our divorce. I want to ask you to forgive me for not being there for you when you were a child. I want to be a part of your life now. Won't you try to forget the past?"

The pain of her childhood was hard to forget. "I don't need you anymore. I needed you when I was a little girl but now I have pulled myself up by my bootstraps and made a life for myself without any help from anyone, except God. My mother is dead and my brother is in prison and I have been on my own for a long time now. When I needed you, you weren't there and that can't be changed with a few sweet words." Tears were in her eyes as she stood and pointed to the door. "Please leave my house. I can't deal with all of this right now." She started sobbing as if her heart would break.

It was at that moment that Michael came up to the open back door and heard her cries. He rushed through the door and went to her side. She raised her head and looked at him and he saw a pain reflected in her eyes that shot right to his heart. "Michael Logan, meet my father James Byron."

Michael didn't respond to the man's outstretched hand. He looked at Melanie's father with a cold look that would strike fear in a man's bones. "It's time for you to leave. If she wants to see you again, we'll let you know." He pointed him to the door.

James started to leave but turned around and laid a piece of paper on the table.

"I'll be staying in town for a few days. I'll just leave the number to my hotel here for her in case she wants to give me a call." He looked back in Melanie's direction. "I'm sorry baby. I've always loved you."

When the door closed Melanie started sobbing uncontrollably. Michael pulled her to his chest and let her cry. He heard the pain in those sobs and he cursed the parents that caused such pain in their only daughter. He couldn't stand to see her like this. This was his Melanie who lit up a room with her smile. He wished he could take her pain upon himself. He just rubbed her back and whispered nonsense words to comfort her. He didn't know what else to do.

After she calmed down they seemed to make an unspoken agreement not to discuss her father. Michael wanted to get her mind off the emotional scene she had been through.

"Miss Melanie, how would you like to go out on a second date with me this evening?"

She looked a little skeptical at the prospect. "I'm hopping on one foot after our first date. I don't know if it's safe to date you or not."

He wasn't doing to take her flimsy excuses and she knew it. "I know we can't really go to a restaurant very easily until you get a little more practice with your crutches. You are supposed to stay off that foot so I had an idea of something we could do. How about going over to my house? I am pretty good at cooking on the grill and we could cook up a couple of steaks and rent a movie on pay per view."

She wasn't sure she was ready to venture out of the house yet because of her foot. She looked over at him and wrinkled her nose. "I don't know Michael because I haven't really been up on my foot much. It is a little painful when I try to walk."

He reached over and took her hand. "That's the romantic part of the date. I get to carry you around wherever you need to go all night. You did say you liked it when I carried you. This is the perfect opportunity to use me as a pack mule."

She giggled at him, "You'd make a really nice looking pack mule but I don't really think that's a romantic image."

He grinned at her and looked a little sheepish. "I'm not very good at the romantic words and images Melanie. You need to cut a guy a little slack."

She reached over and touched his arm. "You do just fine and I'd love to go on a second date with you." She reached over and kissed his cheek. He turned his head and put his finger on his lips. "How about giving me a kiss right here?"

They were still very close and she looked into his eyes and leaned over and gave him a gentle kiss. Michael was very pleased because she had wanted to kiss him. He knew that she was getting used to the idea of them as a couple. He knew she was thinking of him as a man and not just her friend. This was definitely progress.

Late that night after Melanie had gotten home and went to bed, she kept playing the conversation with her father over in her mind. It didn't go very well and she knew she was partially to blame. The emotions just came over her like a dam had burst and a flood was pouring in. He shouldn't have surprised her like that. It was too much of a shock to find him on her doorstep. She thought about the times as a little girl when she had dreamed her daddy would show up and love her again and make their life better. When she saw him it was almost like a flashback of those childish daydreams. What does he want from her now after all these years? He didn't appear to need money. There wasn't anything he could really gain from coming here. She knew she has to get past this hurt before she could move on with her future.

Sunday was a long day for Melanie. She stayed home from church to stay off her foot another day even though she was getting around pretty good on the crutches. She woke up early despite her sleepless night and got out her Bible to do some personal study on her own for the Lord's Day. She turned to a favorite verse that she had learned as a young girl in West Virginia. Psalm 27:10 that says; *when my father and mother forsake me, then the Lord will take me up.* She read on to verse eleven; *teach me thy way, o Lord and lead me in a plain path, because of mine enemies.* She was looking for a plain path and she knew in her heart that the Bible plainly teaches to honor your father and mother. It also teaches forgiveness and praying for those who despitefully use you. Knowing what she should do and being able to do it are two different things.

How could she be an example to teenagers if she couldn't even forgive? Does forgiving mean she has to be best buddies with this man who has caused her so much pain? She knew she didn't have the strength to do this alone so she fell on her knees and prayed for the Lord to help her do the right thing. Crying out to God was something that she knew she could do. She told God exactly how she felt and how she wanted to do the right thing. She asked for the strength and wisdom to be able to do it. When she finished she had a still and peaceful feeling come over her and she knew her prayer had been answered. As Psalm 30:5 says *Weeping may endure for a night, but joy cometh in the morning.*

She decided to call her father and have him over to talk. She wanted someone to be with her but she knew she had to do this alone. She had the Lord and he would give her the strength. She picked up the phone and called the motel where he was staying. He answered on the first ring. She wondered if he had been waiting for her call. She asked him to come over and she sat down on the couch and cuddled her animals. The animals had always been a comfort to her. She had a few minutes to gather her courage.

When James came to the door this time Melanie was prepared to see him. She let him in and they sat down and both of them just remained quiet for a little while. Melanie was stroking her cat Lance as she sat on the couch opposite him. "I will not discuss my mother with you; I just want you to know that before the subject comes up again. I have watched my mother die a painful death from lung cancer and I will always miss her. No matter what you say or do, that will never change."

He didn't respond right away, "I understand how you feel and I will respect your wishes. I'm sorry if anything I said caused you pain." He looked her in the eye and seemed sincere. She spoke the words that had been rolling around in her mind all day, "Exactly what do you want from me? I'm pretty much a grown woman now so we can't go back and relive my childhood. I just can't figure out what you're after."

He rubbed his hands against his slacks nervously, "That's plain talk and I'm not sure I can answer your question. I just want to get to know my children. I want you to tell me about your childhood and what you like to do and if you're happy with your life. I just want to know you."

She looked at him like he had lost his mind, "Why? You've got your own life and so do I. It would be easier to just continue our lives the way they have been."

"I am your father and you can't just pretend I don't exist. We could mean something to each other if you would give me a chance."

She thought about his words and tried to judge their sincerity. "All I can say is I'll try. I can't make any promises. This is very hard for me and I just have to take it one step at a time. Why don't you tell me about your life?"

So he started to talk and he began to tell of his struggles. In order to get over his bad marriage and loosing his children he drifted around the country. He ended up in Richmond and got a job selling cars in a small car lot. He worked hard for a few years and when the owner wanted to retire he bought the business. He did well selling used cars and now has a large car dealership in Richmond. He remained single for several years but five years ago he married a lady he met while selling her a car. He talked about her in a respectful way that made Melanie wonder what she was like. Her name is Sarah and she worked for a bank in Richmond. She had never been married before and didn't have any children.

It was strange learning all these facts about her father. Melanie thought it was like meeting a stranger who wasn't a stranger. She sat there on the couch trying to sort out her emotions because she felt calm and nervous at the same time. It seemed so unreal, seeing this man sitting in her living room and knowing he is her father but feeling so detached from him. She felt God's presence helping her through this. She silently thanked him for his help.

He had stopped talking as if waiting for a reply and she hadn't heard his last sentence. "I have always loved animals. Jerry and I used to escape into the wood so we wouldn't have to deal with the realities of our life. Our life was hard and we struggled just to have food and rent. Sometimes we just did without a lot of things we needed. There were times we didn't have groceries. I remember eating mayonnaise sandwiches because that was all we had. We found happiness in the woods with the animals. As soon as we were old enough we got jobs to help out. There never seemed to be enough money. We learned to work hard and be thankful for what we had. I think having those hard years helped me to realize how blessed I am now. Hardship does make you better if you don't get bitter."

They spent the next two hours catching up on each others lives. As the time passed, the conversation became easier. Melanie found a lot of things that made her who she is, could have come from this man. It was an eye opening experience for her. Around noon there was a knock at her door and as she went to answer it. She found herself a little sad that their time together was over. Feeling that way really surprised her. It was such a confusing turn of events for her.

Helen was at the door and she had brought a casserole for Melanie's lunch. Melanie let her in and introduced her to her father. She hesitated and finally decided on sticking to the simple facts.

She said simply, "Helen this is James Byron." James reached out his hand and Helen shook it. He turned and looked at Melanie, "I guess I'd better go now. I'll call you later." And he was gone leaving nothing but more questions in his absence.

Chapter Fifteen

Melanie's foot had healed nicely and her father had gone back to Richmond. She had agreed to keep in touch via e-mail and phone. They had reached an understanding of sorts. They were like polite strangers who were wary of each other but still curious. Her father seemed reluctant to share too much for fear he might upset her. She has started coming to the realization that this relationship between them would take some time to cultivate. The long distance approach suited her just fine.

Today was an outing with the youth group. They were going to do some community service with some of the shut-ins and elderly of the church. They had agreed to do yard work and any other chores the seniors might need assistance with. It was Saturday and the weather looked like it would be very nice. The kids were to meet at the church and break up into groups of three that would be dropped off at their assigned work place. Melanie was the taxi today.

They had a good turn out with twelve kids showing up at the church. They would have four groups of three. Michael would supervise the yard work and any of the more physical chores they might be asked to do. They would communicate via cell phone. It looked like a wonderful opportunity for the different generations to get to know one another and appreciate one another's gifts.

Melanie ended up with a group of three girls who would be working on Mrs. Parker's flower garden. It used to be her pride and joy but arthritis and immobility had kept her from working in it so far this season. But some of the planting could be done as long as she covered it at night. They had a large garden project on their hands. Mrs. Parker looked pleased as punch as she told the girls about the different plants and flowers and how they needed to be planted and cultivated. Melanie didn't tell her but she learned a lot to help her with her own yard from listening to the conversations with Mrs. Parker.

The community service day was turning into a huge success. Michael was working with Chad, Josh, and John in an elderly couple's yard. They lived out of town a ways in a more rural area. They had a buildup of brush, weeds, and debris at the back of their property from a storm last year. It was a big job and Michael and the boys knew that they would have to really work hard to finish it. The boys were dragging the brush into a pile that would be burned. Michael was using a tool known as a sling blade to chop through the thick weeds. Things were going well and they had cleared most of the area before they had a problem.

Michael was busy working and didn't notice the wet areas around on the ground at his feet. This part of North Carolina has some wet marsh areas that could be a home for a variety of wildlife. Michael was swinging his blade when his arm connected with a snake. He was bitten on the arm. He pulled his arm away and ran from the area. He was pretty sure the snake had been a water moccasin which was extremely poisonous. He had to get the boys out of there. He didn't want them to panic.

Chad was the oldest and most level-headed of the group. He also had his driver's license and he needed to get to the hospital to get an anti-venom shot right away. Michael needed someone with a clear head. He called Chad over and talked to him privately. He decided to play it down for the boy's sake. He told the boy he had been bitten by a snake and had to go have a shot. He was going to call Melanie and have her meet them at the church with the girls. Chad didn't get overly upset but they got the boys into the car quickly. They drove back to the church in record time. They should probably go by ambulance since the nearest hospital was in Southport. He was worried the ambulance would upset the kids but time was very important. He was already starting to feel a little dizzy.

When Melanie got the call she went into a panic. She called the ambulance and had them meet Michael at the church. Her first thought was that she just couldn't loose Michael when she was just getting to know him and care about him. . She also called the pastor so he could be responsible for the children. He didn't seem to understand why she felt that she had to be with Michael. She didn't have time to explain or even know the reason herself. All she knew was she was going with Michael and that was all there was to it.

Her only thought was to get to him as soon as possible. She got the girls together and they rushed back to the church. She put Amber in charge of seeing that everyone got home. She couldn't sit at the church worrying about who had a ride when Michael's life could be hanging in the balance. Chad didn't know what kind of snake it was but Melanie knew t he wouldn't be rushing to the hospital if it wasn't serious. They had to get the anti-venom into him soon.

Michael and the boys were already in the church yard when Melanie and the girls pulled up. The pastor and several other church members were with him and the boys while they waited for the ambulance. Melanie wasn't thinking clearly when she pulled into the parking lot, jumped out of her car and ran to straight to Michael and wrapped her arms around him. Tears were running down her face as she held him for a minute just to feel the comfort of knowing he was alive.

She started touching his face to reassure them both. "What kind of snake, honey?" His voice was hoarse and weak, "A water moccasin got me on the arm." There wasn't time for any more conversation as the ambulance pulled in and the paramedics started running over and working on him.

They loaded him into the ambulance pretty fast and started to the hospital. Melanie didn't take time to talk to anybody except to call out to Amber, "I'm following the ambulance. Take care of the kids and start praying."

She followed behind the ambulance with her flashers on breaking all the speed limits. She had to be there with him when he got to the hospital. It was a scary ride and she was praying all the way there. He had to be alright. She couldn't deal with loosing him. He had become important to her in these last months. Without him her life would be empty. She never felt her life was empty before she started seeing Michael but it must have been because the thought of life without him seemed bleak.

They got to the emergency room and rushed him in. She parked and was steps behind them. When she got to the lobby they wouldn't let her go to him because the doctors were looking at him. She tried to fill out the forms and paced the waiting room. This was the same waiting room he had brought her to a short time ago when he had gotten so worried about her cut foot. Now that she was the one coming with him, she could understand how he had felt a little better. He had to be okay. He was so big and strong that a little snake couldn't possibly have enough venom to kill him. She prayed that they got here in time.

After what seemed like hours but was only minutes, the nurse came out looking for Melanie. Michael was asking for her. She went into the room and he looked very pale and fragile lying on the white sheets. She went to the side of the bed and picked up his hand. He opened his eyes. "Hey beautiful" his voice sounded weak.

Melanie felt tears welling up in her eyes, "Hey good looking, I sure have been worried about you."

He rubbed the back of her hand as if to reassure her, "I'll be fine, it just takes a little while for the anti-venom to work its way through my body. They gave me something to keep me calm too. I'm a little sleepy."

He closed his eyes as he spoke and she smiled. She was so relieved. He would be fine. She breathed a prayer of thanks, "*Thank you God for hearing our prayers.*"

He looked so sweet and cute laying there asleep he reminded her of a little boy. She wondered what his little boys would look like. The thought put a smile on her face as she watched him. He opened his eyes and saw her smiling." Are you looking at me with a smile on your face? Melanie honey, your smile directed at me is a rare and wonderful sight to behold. What are you thinking?"

Her face turned red and she shook her head, "Never mind Mr. Logan. A woman has to have her secrets you know."

He looked at her and wondered if she realized she practically declared her feeling for him in front of half the church. "I don't think that you can hide the fact that you like me from the church members any longer. It looked like you were pretty attached when you came back to the church today."

She remembered how she ran to him in the church yard and blushed. She wondered what this would mean for them as youth leaders who were involved with each other romantically. This could cause Michael to loose his youth group if they thought he was acting inappropriately. She had really done it now. She let her emotions get involved with this man and what a mess they were in.

She watched him sleep and she brushed back the hair from his face. She was thinking that things would have to change now. She would either have to give this wonderful man up or give up being the youth leader. She had experienced first hand how judgmental church members could be, especially when you taught their children. The tongues were most likely wagging right now about how she and Michael were an item and had been teaching the teens together. Her heart was breaking because she knew there was a possibility that Michael would loose his position with the youth which meant so much to him. She had to do something. The question was what could she do to fix this mess?

As Melanie was sitting beside this man she cared for so much holding his hand, his family came into the room. His mother and sister Krystal came rushing in looking worried and upset. His mother rushed to his side and Melanie realized that they belonged there instead of her. She explained he was resting and waiting for the anti-venom to take effect. Melanie knew Michael had family with him to take care of him now so she quietly left the hospital.

She felt like an outsider once again when Michael's family got there. She had gotten too attached to him in such a short time. What was she thinking? She didn't want to be hurt again. She didn't want to hurt him either. She had already ruined his reputation at his church. She was just bad blood as the towns people back home used to say. What made her think she could have a healthy relationship with a good man? She didn't know about good relationships. She had seen too many relationships that had gone bad.

Melanie went home by herself. She didn't want to talk to anybody at the church. She didn't want to think about Michael and how much she had messed up his life. She just wanted to be at home with her animals and think about what she should do now. She had to make some serious decisions and she needed time to think things through. She missed Michael already and she had just left his side.

At the hospital Michael woke up and was looking for Melanie. He looked around the room and saw his mother sitting by his bed where Melanie had been sitting earlier. He was feeling clearer headed all the time and he knew what he wanted most was Melanie there with him." Where's Melanie, mom? Did she go down to the cafeteria?"

His mother looked at him and gave a gentile smile, "She must have left right after we got here, dear. Maybe she had somewhere she had to go."

He digested this information and wondered what had happened to the woman who had acted so loving and concerned just a couple of hours ago. Something must have upset her.

"Did you or Krystal say anything to her to make her feel that she should leave?" He spoke softly but she could tell he was upset.

"Mike, we hardly talked to her when we first arrived and she left without telling us that she planned to go. We would never say anything to make her feel she should leave, you should know that."

He closed his eyes unable to deal with this problem right now. "I know mom, I didn't think you would have said anything to her. She's really sensitive about our relationship because it's so new. She doesn't know where she fits into my life and where I fit into hers. If I get out of this bed any time soon she'll know I want her right beside me for the rest of our lives. She was really worried about me. She even ran up to me in front of several church people and threw her arms around me. It was almost worth being snake bitten. That woman will be my wife if I have anything to do with it."

His mother looked concerned, "Mike just don't rush her. You need to be prepared for the possibility that she might not be ready to get married even if she has feelings for you. Son I don't want you to get your hopes up and be hurt. Why don't you concentrate on getting well right now and then you can worry about your love life."

He was silent but his mind wasn't at rest. He knew Melanie loved him but she just hasn't figured it out yet, today had just confirmed that fact more concretely in his mind. It had been so nice to have her by his side when he needed her. He knew he would always need her and he had to figure out a way to convince her she needed him right back. He couldn't figure out why she left. The last thing he remembered, he was teasing her about how she acted at the church.

Then he realized that was what had set her off. She was upset about what the people at the church would say. She had mentioned something about that before and he had purposed, only half jokingly. She was worried about his reputation. He was a thirty three year old man and he was in love. His reputation was the last thing on his mind. The kids in his youth group weren't dumb. They could see how he felt about her. Why does she think it's wrong to care about one another? The people in this town had known him most of his life. They know he is an honorable man. Why was this woman making everything so complicated? She really was driving him crazy.

Melanie got tired of being alone and called Helen. She owed her a dinner and invited her out for some Mexican food. Helen accepted the invitation and Melanie was on her way over to Helen's house to ride with her when the phone rung. It hurt her to let it ring and not answer it but she knew it was likely to be Michael. She had called the hospital for regular reports and found out they were keeping him overnight just for observation and he would be fine to go home tomorrow. She was so relieved that he was going to be fine. Her heart felt like a big heavy weight in her chest when she thought he might not make it. It took a lot of willpower to leave without answering the phone.

Lance sat on top of the couch and looked at her as if she was crazy. He seemed to know exactly what was going on. Of course Melanie did talk to him like he was a person and not a cat. That might have something to do with the notion that he seems to have about himself being superior to other cats. He had taken a liking to Michael. He must like having another mature male around. Pepe' and Newman couldn't be classified as mature. Sometimes Lance looks like he really wanted to make some sly sarcastic comment. This was one of those times. Newman and Pepe' were unconcerned. The bunny slippers had escaped from the closet shelf. Newman was in for a night of entertainment and Pepe" was excited just to watch. Melanie was glad she still had the boys. They made her a feel little less lonely.

The dinner with Helen was nice. Helen was always good company. She wore a scaled down sombrero type hat with a Mexican looking band around it. For Helen it was tame. The people at the restaurant did look at her a little strange but Melanie found it amusing. She was beginning to see why Helen wore those hats. It made her life interesting and it was pretty funny to see how people reacted.

Melanie just couldn't keep her mind on the conversation. She found her mind wandering every few minutes and Helen was starting to notice that she wasn't herself. She finally broke down and told Helen about the day with Michael and the snake bite. She told her how she had embarrassed them both in the church yard. She confided about the danger of being involved with each other while leading the youth group.

Helen was a good listener. She let Melanie talk to get the burden off her chest. She said a prayer under her breath that she would give this young woman the right advice. When Melanie finished her story, she sat on her side of the table looking miserable and waiting for Helen to reply. Helen took a deep breath and spoke softly.

"Melanie, do you think God knows everything?"

This was not the response that Melanie was looking for so she frowned as he answered, "Of course I do, that's one of the first things I used to teach the children in Sunday School."

"Do you think he knows everything that you and Michael have said and done while you were together?"

"I know he sees all and knows all. He has been with us every second." Melanie was sounding a little irritated.

"Do you have anything you need to ask forgiveness for because of your relationship with Michael?" Helen hoped she could make Melanie see her point.

"No we've never done anything wrong. Michael has a strong faith and he has always been a gentleman." Melanie was starting to see where Helen was going with this.

"Helen, its not God I'm worried about it's the church members. They might think we've been a bad influence on their kids."

Helen looked her in the eye and stated quietly, "Since when do you worry about what some people might think. It's what God thinks that counts. Why don't you and Michael go to the Pastor and see if there is a problem."

Melanie shook her head in refusal, "I don't want Pastor Anthony to have to take sides on this issue. I've been in that situation before and I don't want to go there again."

"Melanie, please don't make the mistake of judging these people by others actions. If you are judging them what makes that better than them judging you?"

They got up to leave and Melanie thought about their conversation as Helen drove home. Was she judging these people unfairly? Could she be wrong about how the church would feel about her and Michael? Somehow she didn't have enough confidence in human nature to believe that Helen might be right.

Chapter Sixteen

Michael would be getting out of the hospital today. He was waiting for the doctor to come and sign his release paperwork. He was pacing his room like a caged tiger. He wanted to get out of here. He had to see Melanie. He tried to call her several times last night and she didn't answer. He knew something was wrong but he just wasn't sure what it was. His doctor was expected two hours ago. If he didn't show up soon, Michael was leaving without any paperwork. He felt fine today and this red tape was a waste of his time. Even though it was Sunday he knew Melanie wouldn't go to church. She would be too embarrassed about yesterday. Michael needed to talk to her and reassure her before she talked herself into doing something crazy. He knew how unreasonable she could be at times.

The doctor finally showed up and Mrs. Logan drove Michael home. She had intended to stay at his house and take care of him the rest of the day. When they pulled into the driveway Michael jumped out like a man with a purpose. "Thanks for the ride and everything, mom. You're the best." He went into his house and closed the door leaving a bewildered mother sitting in her car. He wanted a shower and some clean clothes before he saw Melanie and then you could bet he would be at her house as soon as he could get there. He didn't even realize his mother had planned to stay because he was so focused on his plan.

Melanie had made a decision in the early morning hours. She was getting up and driving to the prison in West Virginia to see Jerry today. Since the shop was closed on Monday, if she got an early start this morning, she should be able to make the trip there and back in time to get a little sleep and open the shop on Tuesday. She needed to see her brother. Her life seemed to be in such a mess and he would help her make sense of it all. She didn't tell anyone where she was going. She just left plenty of food and water for the boys and threw a few things in a bag and left.

She had made the trip a few times now and she knew the best roads to take. It took about eight hours of driving time one way. Since she left at five in the morning, she could be at the prison in time for visiting hours and then find a motel to rest and drive back tomorrow. The only thing that concerned was if Old Yeller was mechanically sound enough to make the long trip.

Since Michael's friend the mechanic checked the car out a couple of months ago, Melanie hadn't really done any more maintenance to it. Jerry had always taken care of the car for her. She still hadn't trained herself to be a car guy and never worried about what might go wrong or what a noise could mean. She just went to the quick oil place and filed her up with gas. She was hoping that Old Yeller would make it without any problems. Michael would probably have a fit when he found out she struck out for such a long trip without checking on the car first. It was an older model but it had been well taken care of.

Melanie spent her driving time listening to her praise music and praying. She wanted to be sure that she was listening if God were to give an answer to her question about what to do. She had never heard an audible voice but she had sure been given some answers before in various ways. When she was seeking God about coming to North Carolina she had been reading her Bible when she came upon a verse in Isaiah 30:21 that said, *"This is the way, walk ye in it."* It might have been part of a Psalm but she knew the Lord had made those words jump out at her. She had many other instances when she knew she was being answered but this time all she heard was confusion and silence. She knew confusion was not what God had for her but she couldn't seem to stop herself from being confused.

Should she resign as youth leader or should she break up with Michael? These seemed to be her two choices. Either way it would hurt them both. She knew after much soul searching that she had fallen in love with that big frustrating man. The knowledge did not make her happy at all but scared her silly. Love could be so painful. She thought about her parents and how they were both so hurt from the divorce along with her and Jerry. She thought about Jerry and his love for Rachel. How could love for a woman have brought him to such a terrible place as prison? She really didn't know anybody in her family that she could say she would want to model a marriage after.

What had happened to her well thought out plans? She had worked so hard to get her cottage by the sea and her pet shop. She just wanted a quiet life to enjoy them. Now it seemed like her plans weren't enough anymore. Why couldn't she just be happy with what she had accomplished? Why did she want this sweet wonderful aggravating man in her life? Why did she have this deep felt need to work with these teens?

She had seen such a drastic change in Autumn since she started working at the shop. She had come to a couple of youth group meetings now and Melanie knew that she was close to making a commitment to God and becoming part of the group. How could that be wrong?

Melanie drove straight through and arrived at the prison for the Sunday 2:00 visiting time. She signed up at the guardhouse and found out her brother already had a visitor registered for today. It was her father James. She had no idea he was still visiting Jerry regularly. She was glad that Jerry had some family to come and see him but she had really wanted to talk to him alone today or as alone as you can get in a prison visitor's room. She would just have to talk to Jerry in front of her father. She hadn't driven all this way not to be able to see and talk to her brother. She needed to feel the closeness they always shared. She needed to feel like somebody was in her corner.

She sent into the room and sat at a table. Her father was also shown into the room and sat at the table with her. It was a little awkward before Jerry was led out and allowed to join them. She wasn't permitted to hug him but as he sat across the table from her she took his hand and looked into his eyes as she felt the tears come into hers. He nodded toward their father.

"Hey Mel, what are you doing here? Couldn't stay away from West Virginia?"

She smiled at him and rubbed his hand, "I just felt an overwhelming need to see you. I got up early this morning and drove down."

"I am glad you did, you look real good sis. It's so good to see you." He looked over at James, "I'm glad to see you too don't get me wrong but it's been months since I've seen Melanie."

James nodded his head in agreement, "I was surprised to see her today myself. It was a happy surprise though. You two go ahead and visit, don't mind me, I'll just sit here and watch my two kids together. It's the first time in a lot of years that I can say that." He leaned back in his chair and smiled.

Melanie turned back to Michael, "I have gotten myself into a fix back at the beach. I have been dating this man."

"Hold it right there, are you sure this is my sister Melanie talking? You've been dating a man? You told me about a friend in your letters but I had no idea it had progressed to a dating stage."

"Well it has and I actually think I'm in love with him,"

"My big sister Melanie the girl who had the reputation for punching any suitors in the nose is in love. Will wonders never cease? I am happy for you, girl."

"There's no need to be happy for me because I have messed the whole thing up and I'm miserable." She stuck out her bottom lip like she used to when she was a little girl and grinned at him.

Then she began to share with them about her relationship with Michael, the youth group, the church members and her dilemma. She talked for at least ten minutes non-stop but had both men's undivided attention. She also had the attention of a couple of guards trying to act like they weren't listening. She was a great story teller. She started with the breakdown of her car and told a little about how they came to care for each other ending with the incident at church with the snake bite and her leaving him at the hospital.

Jerry looked confused, "What's the problem Mel? He sounds like a great guy and you two could be really happy together."

She burst into tears, "Why should I believe that we can be happy? Who do we know that's had a good happy marriage? I am scared of the whole thing. I'm scared of the church people asking us to step down, I'm scared that I'm not capable of having a good relationship, I'm scared of loving someone and getting hurt."

At this point James slid his chair closer to hers and put his arm around her shoulders. "Baby, don't cry, you're a great girl and that man would be lucky to have you. You can't judge everyone else by your mother and I or even Jerry and Rachel. My parents were married for forty seven years before my father passed away. My mother died less than a year later because she loved him so much she didn't want to live anymore. You might not remember them but you kids went with us to see them a couple of times when you were little. I have a great wife now and we are very happy together. And as for the church folk, it's not a sin to fall in love honey. God is love and he tells us it's not good for a man to be alone. That goes for a woman too."

Jerry picked up her hand and brought it to his lips. "Mel, I am so sorry you feel this way. I feel I'm partly to blame for all your pain and fear. I want you to know that even if I could go back and live that time over again with Rachel, I'd still love her and marry her and do my best to protect her. Love is worth the pain. You're the one who always told me about the pain Jesus went through for us. If you love someone you'll give anything even your life for them. I'm not sorry that I loved Rachel even though I'm here in prison. Don't be afraid to love that man Melanie. You deserve to find happiness."

Tears fell from her eyes and she decided she needed to give Jerry something positive for this visit. "Hey little brother, did I tell you about the time the monkey let the gerbils loose in the shop?" And with that the conversation about her love life was over and before she left she had Jerry and her father rolling in laughter.

She found out her father had hired a new attorney for Jerry and his case would be coming up for appeal soon. This attorney thought he could get a reduction in Jerry's sentence. That was certainly exciting news. Something about this news changed Melanie's feelings about her father and his motives. They had a nice time together despite the surroundings. Melanie was glad that she had come. She was even going to have dinner with her father. He would even get her a room in the really nice motel. It was at the same one where he was staying. She thought she could handle a little one on one time with her father tonight now she had seen Jerry. Especially since her father was trying to help him get out of prison.

They left the prison together and he walked her to her car. They had agreed she would follow him to the motel and so they could freshen up and rest before dinner. When she got into her car and turned the key nothing happened. Old Yeller just wouldn't even turn over. This was bad. What would she do now?

James got out of his nice new car and came to her window. "Melanie, pop the hood and let's see what's wrong." He opened the hood and what he saw caused him a lot of concern. "Melanie, did you check the oil since you left home? It looks like your oil has gotten pretty low and your engine block has cracked."

Melanie had no idea what that meant. "Can you fix it?" She needed her car to get home. He shook his head negatively, "I'm afraid your little car has a blown motor." She didn't know what she was going to do now. She had to have a car to function. She couldn't even get to the shop. She had used most of her savings with the move and opening the shop. She was in a terrible fix so she called on the only one who could help her. *"Lord I need some help. A new car would be nice but right now I'd settle for a ride to the motel."*

James opened her car door and held out his hand. "Come on Mel, I'll drive you to the motel and we'll see what we can do about towing the car to a garage." She got her bag and followed him silently. She was in a daze from the early morning and the long drive and all the emotions she had been bottling up. She was only too happy to let her father help out with a tow.

Back in Long Beach, Michael was a frantic man. He had no idea where Melanie could have gone. He called everyone he could think of and the only one that had heard from her was Autumn. She has called and asked her to feed the animals at the shop. Melanie hadn't told Autumn where she was going but she had told her she'd be back to work on Tuesday.

If he could find her right now he'd be tempted to kiss her senseless and wring her neck at the same time. This woman was driving him crazy all right. He'd hurried through his shower as soon as his mother had dropped him off that morning. Then he had rushed over to Melanie's house and found her gone. No car, no note. She had not told Helen that she was going anywhere. He did find out that they had dinner together last night. Helen told him that she had been a little upset but she was sure that it would all work out. She was going to help out with the shop if she was needed but between Autumn and the young man Melanie had hired, it was all taken care of. No matter what he asked her she wasn't volunteering any more information than that. If Michael could just be sure that she was all right.

That sardine can of a car she drove, could break down at any time. He knew she was a little upset but if he could just talk to her, he knew that he could calm her fears. He hated the thought of her driving around all upset but to look for her would be foolish. She could be anywhere. There were so many things in North Carolina she had told him she would like to see. He planned to take her to those places as soon as they got this little bump in the road smoothed out. He couldn't do anything else but go home and pray and that was exactly what he did. He asked God to protect her and to have her call and let him know she was all right. He had to rest on his faith now and believe she would be fine and he would see her on Tuesday. In the meantime he was staying close to the phone just in case.

James was sorry about Melanie's car but he knew he could help her out if she'd allow him to. After all, he owned a car dealership and getting her a car to drive wouldn't be that difficult for him. He had a friend at the Columbia dealership that he could call and work out something. That little yellow Volkswagen had seen its better days but James still wanted to get it fixed for her because he knew she really loved it. He started making some calls. The hard part would be convincing Melanie to let him help her. She was a fiercely proud little thing.

Melanie was pacing in her room. She was frantic with worry. She had to come up with a plan. She felt like she had to do something and forgot about trusting God in the situation.

Chapter Seventeen

James and Melanie met in the hotel lobby to go to dinner. They had decided on a trendy chain restaurant that they were both familiar with. Melanie was still walking around in a fog wondering how she would get home. She had decided to ask her father to help her get on a bus back to North Carolina. She would try to find a place that might buy her beloved car because she just couldn't invest the money in that Old Yeller right now when she needed a dependable vehicle to drive every day. She was sad to loose Old Yeller but she knew there was no way she could afford to get it towed home or repaired any time soon. She planned to scrape enough cash up to try to put a down payment on an economy car.

James had other plans for Melanie and her car. He had found someone to tow it to a garage that would repair it. It might take a while to get the needed parts but he told them he wanted it repaired and restored and they could wait for the job to be done right. He had made a deal with his Buddy at the Saturn dealership and he had traded a vehicle from his lot to this guy in Columbia for a 2005 Saturn with a convertible top and a nice gold paint job. It was the best he could do on such short notice but he was pleased. He wanted to make the car a gift to Melanie, but would she accept it? If she insisted on paying for it he would set up some payments on a ridiculously small amount. He was betting she had no idea what cars cost a dealer and he would keep it that way. He had never been able to help his daughter before but he was now.

They were seated at the table in the restaurant when he brought up the subject. "Melanie, I have something in mind to help you with your car situation and I want you to hear me out before you decide." Tears of worry came into her eyes but she took a drink of her sweet iced tea and nodded her consent. "I have a friend who has a car dealership here in Columbia that I do some business with. I have made a really good deal on a car that he has. It might work out for you. Now I know you are worried about paying for it but I really want you to let me make it a gift. I never had the chance to give you Christmas or birthday gifts when you were a little girl. I didn't get to teach you to drive or help you get your first car. I really want you to let me give you this car."

Melanie took her finger and drew a circle in the water that had collected on the table from her glass. She realized that all her plans were for nothing. God had this whole thing under control. She was quiet for a few minutes and then she looked him in the eye and said, "Okay, I'll take it. I don't want you to think I'm going to be picky or anything but what kind of car is it?"

He let out a sign of relief, "Its gold 2005 Saturn convertible and it's got a really low amount of miles on it."

She smiled a smile that lit up the room. "I expected some kind of large sedan that looked like a grandma car. I really didn't have any idea it would be anything so nice. It really is too much for a gift."

"Nothing is too good for my little girl. I don't want to have to worry every time you get out on the road. I also found someone to tow in your Volkswagen. I'll take care of that for you."

"Just sell it for parts or whatever you can get. Thank you Pop." This was he first time she had called him anything because she wasn't sure what to call him. When she heard Jerry call him Pop it somehow seemed to fit. James felt like he had just been handed a million dollars. He smiled at her and picked up the menu. "Do you know what you want to eat?

Later that night Melanie was back in her room thinking about Michael. She had to find out if he made it home all right and if he was recovering from his snake bite. She couldn't stand to go another day without talking to him so even though it was after eleven o'clock she picked up the phone and dialed his number.

He answered on the third ring because he had fallen asleep in the chair watching television. "Hello"

Melanie was so glad to hear his voice. "Hey Michael, how are you?" His emotions were on the surface as he answered her, "I'm lonely and worried and needing to talk to my woman. That's how I am."

She smiled at his response, "I need to talk to you too. But first tell me how your feeling. I've been so worried about you."

"You could have fooled me. Why did you leave me in the hospital Melanie? I woke up and you were gone."

"When your family came I didn't feel like I belonged there anymore. I don't know Michael I got a little crazy when you got hurt. I didn't handle it very well."

"Melanie you belong with me no matter who else is around. I need you by my side in the hard times of life along with the good times."

"I just have a hard time with this relationship stuff and it's difficult for me to explain. I hope you'll forgive me for leaving you in the hospital, but I want you to know that I didn't leave until I knew you were going to be fine. I even called to check on you several times after I left. I was worried about you and I care very much what happens to you."

"That's good to hear honey, I was beginning to think you had skipped town and weren't coming back."

"I wouldn't do that Michael. I came home to West Virginia to see Jerry. I drove up early this morning. I really needed to see him."

He released a sigh of relief just to know where she was. "Did you make it okay and get in to see him today?"

"I made it here fine and my father is here too. We had a wonderful visit with Jerry and I'm really glad I came. I thought I might have a bit of a problem getting home though. I guess I drove Old Yeller to death. Her block cracked and her motor blew."

Michael jumped up out of the chair and started walking toward the bedroom to change clothes. "I'll get up right now and come get you Melanie. Where are you? Are you in a safe place?"

"I'm fine Michael, don't worry. I told you my father is here and God has really provided for me. I'm staying in a very nice motel. It's so fancy there's candy in the pillow and a mask to put over your eyes when you go to sleep. I wish you could see it and the best part is the way God has worked things out for me by using my father."

Michael relaxed and sat back down." That's great honey; I wish I could be there to see it too." Michael got stuck on the comment of her wishing he was there with her. She must still want to be with him and that was good news for him.

"He has gotten another car for me. It's practically new and he's giving it to me as a gift. I have decided to accept it even though it's a hard thing for me to do. He told me that he hadn't been able to give me gifts for most of my childhood and he wanted to try to make up for that by doing this for me. He owns a car dealership back in Richmond and apparently has some connections."

"When can you get the car?"

"I'm supposed to go look at it and he's going to close the deal tomorrow if I like it."

"What kind of car is it?"

"It's a 2005 Saturn and it's a convertible and it's gold! I'm very excited. I've never really had a nice car before. I've just had to settle for whatever I could pay cash for."

"That sounds perfect for you honey and I'm happy for you. I'm happy for me too because I'll be able to stop worrying about you breaking down every time you go somewhere. When will you be home?"

She thought about it for a few minutes. "I might not make it tomorrow night. I think I should call and see if Helen could open the shop on Tuesday. I don't want to have to rush through this thing with my father tomorrow. It might be best if I start driving tomorrow evening and stop somewhere and rest and finish the trip on Tuesday. Will you go by my house and check on the boys?"

"I'll take care of the boys for you and I'll call Helen and get her to open the shop. I think it sounds like a good idea for you to take your time coming back even if it means I won't get to see you as soon.

You'll be driving an unfamiliar car and you need to allow a little extra time."

They talked a little longer until Melanie started yawning and Michael remembered they both had a full day tomorrow. He hated to hang up because he didn't want to loose this close feeling they had shared while they talked on the phone. He reluctantly told her good night and he was finally able to get some rest knowing that she was all right. Melanie fell asleep almost as soon as her head hit the pillow.

The next day Melanie woke up feeling a little lost. She was not used to having to depend on others for anything. Having to depend on her father to help her get back home and get herself another car was something that made her feel funny. She felt like a new page had turned in their relationship. Knowing he was working so hard to get Jerry out of jail meant the world to her and now him helping her out of this jam and buying a car for her. That was a huge deal to her. She realized he really did want to be a father to them and that's exactly what he had done yesterday. It was a strange but a good feeling. She had a father who had been there for her when she needed him. Now that was a new and wonderful blessing to her. She got up and dressed and went to meet her father for breakfast. It was a big day for them both.

The car was shiny as a new penny and looked like something Melanie would have chosen for herself. She couldn't be more pleased. After they got the insurance and license plate taken care of, Melanie and James walked back outside where the salesman had pulled the car out front. James smiled like he was the one receiving a gift and handed her the keys. She was so excited that she threw her arms around him and hugged him. It was a wonderful moment for them both. This experience had brought such a healing and restoration process to them. It had to have been part of God's plan all along.

Melanie threw her bag in the back and put the top down. She was smiling from ear to ear as James stood and watched her drive away. She found some good music on the radio and pointed her new car in the direction of the interstate. Her heart felt full right now and she was going to enjoy the feeling. She knew she still had to deal with Michael and the church gossip and whatever else faced her back home but right now she was going to stop and praise the Lord. She could be riding a smelly old bus home right now with no means of transportation when she got there, but instead she was driving this beautiful car. Life is good and she knew she was a blessed woman.

Michael was back at home trying to take care of anything that might be a problem for her when she got there. The boys as she chose to call those spoiled animals of hers, were not too happy about being left behind. It looked like they had taken their frustration out on a roll of toilet tissue. Pepe' and Newman were still having a wonderful time with the pieces that were all over the house when Michael arrived that morning. Melanie's clean little house looked like a bachelor pad after a wild party. These animals had been having themselves a grand old time. Michael started to work cleaning up the mess. Lancelot sat perched on the sofa as if watching the whole scene in grand amusement. Michael rubbed his head when he passed by the couch. It took him almost two hours to get the house back in shape. He vacuumed and swept up pieces in almost every inch of the house. Then he tried to put the other things that he discovered back to normal. He found a bedroom slipper in the dog food dish and a piece of what looked like it might be an ear from a stuffed animal on Melanie's bed. It was an interesting morning for him.

Helen was having her own wild day at the shop. Felix had been cooped up all weekend so Helen thought she would let him have some free time. She let him out of his habitat and was trying to fasten his collar around his neck when he used his long tail to spring himself up on the highest shelve in the back of the store. He had made himself at home dancing around up there and Helen had been trying to catch him the rest of the morning. When she got busy with customers, he would go back to the other animals and try to open the cages. He was being a bit mischievous to say the least and Helen had decided to call in reinforcements. She was expecting Autumn any minute now and hoped that between the two of them they could out fox that crazy monkey.

Melanie had no clue about any of this and she was taking a leisurely drive back home in her new car. She had seen a large mall from the interstate and decided to stop and shop a little. She found herself a knockout outfit she couldn't wait to wear if she could find some occasion to wear it. She had also gotten a gift for Helen for being so kind in helping out at the store. She found her a fabulous hat. Melanie did pay her a small wage but she knew Helen didn't need money. She was doing this for friendship and that was so wonderful of her. She wanted to get a gift for Michael but couldn't find anything that she wanted to give him. She ended up getting him a small stuffed Tweedy Bird just as a joke gift to remind him of her.

By late evening she found a place to stay that was close to the interstate with a nearby restaurant. She spent the evening quietly watching television and thinking about what she would do about Michael and the youth group. She had decided she would resign as the female leader so that maybe the church would let Michael continue in his position. It seemed like the best solution to the problem. She had made a major decision about Michael. She was going to keep him. She wasn't going to let this or anything else, force her to break up with him. She knew if she did she wouldn't only break his heart but her own because she knew she was in love with the man. She didn't think she would let him know that just yet though. He might get too sure of himself if she did. She did think she'd give him a call just to hear his voice before she went to sleep. Something about talking to him made her relax and feel good inside.

The phone only rang once when she heard him breathlessly answer it. "Hey Michael, how are you feeling?"

"I'm feeling much better since you called me. Are you on the way home yet?"

"I'm more than half way and I stopped and got myself a room. It's not nearly as nice as the one that my father got me in Columbia but it's clean and comfortable."

"How do you like your new car? Does it drive all right?"

"Oh Michael it drive like a dream. I've been floating down the road in it. I absolutely love it."

He smiled hearing the excitement in her voice. "So when are you going to take me for a ride in that new car of yours?"

She thought about it a minute and knew she'd see him as soon as she could after getting back to town. "How about I pick you up tomorrow night at seven o'clock? You can feed me dinner and I'll supply the transportation. We need to take the puppy over for Laura too. Let's go by there first."

"Sounds like a plan to me, honey. I can't wait to see you."

"I miss you Michael, I hope you know that. How did you get so ingrained into my life that I miss you after a couple of days? That can't be good."

He chuckled at her teasing, "It sounds pretty good to me because I feel the same way." She tried to sound disgusted about the whole thing, "Well at least we're in this together."

"You can say that again Miss Melanie."

"I guess I'd better hang up now. My calling card is running out of minutes. I will see you tomorrow night Mr. Logan."

"I'll be ready with bells on. Goodnight sweetheart."

"Goodnight Michael."

Chapter Eighteen

Melanie made it home and was very happy to see her little house by the sea. It felt like home to her now. She was also really happy to see the boys. They looked pretty happy to see her too. They must have been worried she wouldn't be back. She found the house suspiciously neat and clean for those three rascals to have been there alone for two days amusing themselves. She wondered if Michael had something to do with it. She was so glad to be home that she just sat in her kitchen and enjoyed a cup of coffee with the boys close by her side. She knew she needed to check on Helen at the shop and see how things had been going. She also knew she should figure out what she would wear on her date with Michael tonight but instead she decided to take a walk on the beach. She got Pepe's leash and snapped it on before they went outside just in case Peaches was in the vicinity. They stepped outside into the spring sunshine together and she breathed a prayer of thanks.

"Thank you Lord for taking care of me, even when I was resisting you all the way. It's so nice to have an earthly father that seems to love me and want to be good to me. It's so nice to have my dreams come true with my little house by the sea and my little shop. The extra desires of my heart are what make my heart burst into praise. Michael is the love of my life. He's been trying to tell me that but I was being stubborn. I want to marry him and have his children some day. The thoughts of what a blessing it is to be thinking that, I Melanie Byron might have children is so awesome. I was the poor

little girl from the wrong side of the tracks that people wouldn't walk down the street with. Now I am a property owner and a respected business woman and I am in love with a wonderful man. God you are truly amazing to have taken my life and done something with it. I can never thank you enough for loving me and giving me a new life in you. Amen."

Melanie walked along the shore and was thinking about Michael and what she could do to make this a special night for them. She wanted to tell him she loved him but she was thinking maybe she should tell him another thing or two that he might like. All of the sudden, she was excited to get home and make plans. She would check in on the store and then she would start getting her plans made. Everything should be special.

Melanie got back to the house and a surprise was awaiting her. A delivery van was leaving her driveway and her neighbor Mr. Johnson was holding a box. When she came walking up he smiled at her. He was a retired banker who moved to the beach from Boston, with his wife to enjoy the warm climate. He was smiling at her as she approached. She had such a serene smile on her face and Mr. Johnson was thinking about how lovely she looked today.

She was day dreaming of Michael and how she was going to surprise him tonight. The sunflowers made her smile and she knew exactly who they were from this time. The card said one simple line "love always, Michael." That stinker beat her to the declaration of love but she still had one little surprise up her sleeve.

Melanie called the shop and Helen said not a word about the mishap with Felix. She knew that Melanie had been sorting out her family problems and she had eventually taken care of the monkey problem. She and Autumn had managed to wrangle the little guy and get him back into his habitat. She learned a new lesson about dealing with the animals that Melanie had forgotten to share with her. If all else fails use food as bait. A banana was all it took to get Felix to settle down and go back into his habitat. All the begging and calling Helen had tried was a waste of time. Everything was quiet in the shop now and it had really been a rather slow day for customers. She was glad Melanie had made it home safe and she had made peace with her father at last. Helen knew that her prayers for Melanie had been answered and she couldn't be more pleased. Now if that girl would just grab that nice young man before he got away.

Melanie dressed with care for her evening with Michael. She wore the new outfit she had bought at the mall on the way home from West Virginia. It was a very flattering pantsuit that looked great with her hair and eyes. She felt pretty in it and she had learned that feeling like you look pretty was important. She realized she had bought more clothes for herself since she met Michael than she had in the whole six months before that. Having a man around could be expensive. She tucked one of her sunflowers behind her ear and checked her appearance in the mirror and grabbed her bag as she walked out the door. She took a deep breath and prayed for courage. Tonight was a big night for them both.

Melanie went by the shop and picked up the puppy for Laura. That little girl would be so excited. Melanie had told Krystal the puppy would be ready to pick up today but since she was away from the shop, she offered to deliver it herself. She really wanted to see that cute little girl's face when she saw her puppy for the first time.

Michael was sitting on the porch at his house waiting, not too patiently, for Melanie to drive up. He had a lot to tell her tonight. He had talked to Pastor Anthony about the youth group and the fact that he and Melanie were dating. The pastor didn't have a problem with it at all. They decided that if any parents had a problem they would talk to them about how having a good example of how to date could be an excellent way to show them how a Christian couple should conduct themselves. It wasn't a problem for any of the parents that they were aware of and there was no reason Melanie or Michael should resign as the youth leaders. As far as he was concerned there was no problem but convincing Melanie of that fact could prove to be a challenge. He knew that if she would admit it to him or not, she had considered breaking up with him because of the embarrassment at the church. He didn't want her doing something like that because of the youth group. As much as he wanted her to help with the kids, he wanted her to be in his life much more.

Melanie pulled up into the driveway and he went out the see her new car. He rubbed his hand along the hood. "This is very nice Melanie. I wouldn't mind cruising around town with a beautiful woman in this car at all." She frowned up at him from her driver's side window, "Your not driving around in this car with anybody but me."

He chuckled as he went around to the passenger's side and got in. "You are the beautiful woman that I was referring to Miss Melanie." He leaned over the console of the car and kissed her a brief hello kiss. "I have missed you so much."

She brought his face back to hers and kissed him again. "I have really missed you too." He had a bemused look on his face as she grinned at him and backed out of the driveway.

Melanie glanced into the back of the car. "I have the puppy in a carrier in the back seat. She is sleeping right now. Are you ready to make a special little girl very happy?"

"Michael was looking forward to giving the puppy to his niece but he really wanted to talk to Melanie right now. He knew it would be better to go along with her plans for the evening but it was hard for him to not be in control. This was an area in his life that God was still working on. Melanie had done a lot to help him grow in this area of his personality but she just didn't know it. He was starting to like the surprises that come along with letting her plan their time together.

They arrived at Krystal and David's house and Melanie got the carrier from the back seat. Michael had not seen the puppy for a few weeks and he was pleasantly surprised at how it had turned into such a cute little thing. He knew Laura was going to fall in love with this puppy. She was so cute with her face that resembled a teddy bear and her longish hair that looked a little silver on her back. Melanie was right about this being the perfect puppy for Laura.

Laura was standing beside her mother when she answered the door. Michael had called and let them know that they were bringing the puppy by this evening. He was carrying a bag of supplies that Melanie had put together that the puppy would need. Melanie had the small pet carrier in her arms.

"What's in that Uncle Mike? Her voice sounded hopeful and excited. "Did Miss Melanie bring her cat to visit us?" Laura remembered the stories Melanie had told them about her cats in Sunday School.

Michael held back his smile. "Nope, it's not a cat, baby girl. It's something for a very special little person."

Laura started jumping up and down in her excitement. "Is it my very own puppy that I prayed for Uncle Mike? I knew that God was going to answer my prayer for my very own puppy but I didn't know he would have you to bring it to me."

Michael smiled at her and Melanie came forward and set the cage down on the porch. She reached inside and got the little puppy out for the little girl's inspection. Laura looked up at her mother. "Can I have her for my very own Mommy? Can she live with me in my room and everything?"

Krystal knelt down beside the little puppy and picked her up. "It looks like she might have to live in your room since she is so little. She'll have to stay in her carrier when your not holding her until she learns to be potty trained." She handed the puppy to her daughter and the little girl looked at her in awe.

"This is the prettiest puppy that I ever saw. I already know her name. It's Sassy."

She reached down and kissed the little puppy and the puppy licked her cheek. It was love at first sight.

Michael and Melanie didn't stay and visit. They explained that they had plans and were on their way as soon as Melanie finished explaining to Laura the importance of taking good care of her puppy. She offered to give her some obedience training in a few weeks after the puppy got settled with her new family. Delivering the puppy was very nice but both of them had other things on their minds tonight.

Melanie was pulling out of Krystal's driveway when she paused and nervously licked her lips and looked over at Michael. Now it was time to set her plan into motion. If things worked out the way she hoped she would be engaged by the end of this night. Her heart started racing and her palms were getting sweaty. She prayed that her courage wouldn't fail her now when she needed it the most.

"If it's all right with you I thought we'd take a little walk on the beach before we have dinner, I want to talk to you about something." Michael didn't like the sound of that. He knew that she had been spending a lot of time thinking about their relationship. He hoped she hadn't changed her mind about him. But then again she had just kissed him that was a good sign. You just never could tell with his Melanie. She was always keeping him guessing. He knew one thing for sure; he wouldn't give up on their relationship without a fight.

They pulled in to a deserted beach access road and parked. It was just about twilight and it was part of Melanie's plan to walk on the beach at sunset. Michael got out and went around opening the door for her. He reached for her hand and noticed how nice she looked. "Honey you are a knock-out tonight. I am a lucky man."

She didn't reply because she was trying to figure out how to get to the subject she desperately wanted to talk about. She grabbed his hand and started walking along the shore and watching the waves. The ocean always made her calmer. That was one reason she wanted to come here tonight. "Michael, I've been thinking."

He was wondering where she was going with this and he tried to keep it light. "That's always dangerous." He grinned over at her.

"I'm serious now, I've been thinking about our relationship and I think it should change." This was sounding worse by the minute to Michael. "What do you think needs to change honey; I think we're great together."

She looked over at him and guessed his thoughts, "I don't want to break up if that's what you're thinking. I want to ask you something."

"Melanie, you can ask me for anything and I'd do my best to give it to you. I love you."

I love you too but I want you to hush and let me ask you this." His face broke out into a big smile. "You love me huh? Well it would have been nice if you'd have told me a little sooner."

Hush, I'm trying to ask you something." Her sweet face was deep in concentration. "Do you remember the first time the kids saw us together and I was worried about what people thought?" He nodded his head in consent, "Sure I remember every minute we've spent together."

162

Do you remember what you told me that day?" Michael thought back to the day shortly after he realized how much he loved her. "I remember telling you that we should get married and you punched me on the arm."

"Well I've changed my mind and I am asking you Michael Logan, the man of my dreams, to marry me and let me be your woman forever." They stopped walking at the same time and she looked up at him. She let out the breath that she had been holding and reached up to stroke his face.

He found his voice and reached for her. "Let me get this straight, you are proposing to me?" Their faces were nearly touching and she nodded. He grinned that little boy grim at her that made her heart skip a beat. "And you are offering to be my woman forever?" She nodded again and smiled slightly because she could see the love in his eyes.

You Melanie Byron are the woman of my dreams and I have been waiting for God to send you to me for a long time. It would be the happiest day of my life on the day that you would finally be my wife. I gladly accept your proposal but I want you to know that I intend to do the asking one more time when I put my ring on your finger. You are a lady of surprises and I look forward to being surprised by you many times in the future.

Then he picked her up and swung her around and kissed her with all of the emotions that he had been holding back for so long. She kissed him right back. The happiness Melanie felt there that night on the beach almost overwhelmed her. She knew that this was right and that God had blessed them with these feelings. Now they could plan a future together with God in the center of their lives.

He put her down and they looked at each other and he kissed her again. She broke off the kiss and pushed him slightly. "Hold on there love, we aren't married yet. I plan on a long engagement so that we can have plenty of time to get to know each other and plan our life together." She looked up at him to gage his reaction. "Honey whatever you want is fine with me. I am in favor of a long engagement as long as we set a definite date and work towards our future together."

Okay, what do you say you buy me some dinner and we'll talk about it?" She started to turn back in the direction of the car. "Just a minute Melanie, there is one more thing that I need to hear from you before we leave." She furrowed her brow trying to imagine what it could be. "What do you need to hear darling?"

He pulled her back into his arms. "Well calling me darling is a good start but I need to hear three other words from you right now." She finally realized what he was talking about. "I love you Michael Logan. I love you very much and I always will."

He hugged her to himself and felt the tears start to well up in his eyes. "Those would be the words. I love you too Miss Melanie and now I'm going to buy you the best dinner that we can find in this town." They walked back to the car arm in arm and didn't even feel the sand beneath their feet because they were both walking on air.

Epilogue

Had it been two years since Melanie and Michael had been married? It seemed like yesterday. Today was their second anniversary and Melanie had just finished the best year of her life so far. She knew that she and Michael had their whole life ahead of them and she expected that it wouldn't always be perfect but together they could handle whatever this life had in store for them.

Melanie was sitting on the couch in the new house that Michael had built for her on the ocean. She looked out the window at the beautiful garden she and Michael had planted together. They had been like those flowers and their relationship had bloomed into something beautiful. It hadn't always been perfect, they sometimes disagreed. They tried to remember the rule that they should not let the sun go down on their anger. Together they were building the life that they had planned.

She was holding the remote control and as she pushed the play button the pictures came up on the screen and the memories of their wedding came flashing across her mind like a movie.

The simple but elegant wedding on the beach had been a dream-come-true for them both. James had walked Melanie down the aisle and it was a special moment between the two of them. The small group that had gathered there to witness the event had included an unexpected guest. Her brother Jerry had gotten parole sooner than anyone had expected and had shown up to make the day the more special than Melanie could have imagined. It was like a dream now as she watched her wedding video. Helen had ordered her dress from New York. It was a simple but elegant tea length gown in organdy and lace. She had a worn a Tierra and her hair had been put up with ringlets of curls cascading down her face. She had been a beautiful bride.

Michael had worn an elegant black tux. Melanie remembered thinking that he was the handsomest man that she had ever seen. They had decided to include the youth group in the wedding so the praise band had furnished the music and Autumn had surprised them all by having an excellent singing voice. She sang a love song that brought tears to a lot of eyes that day. Tears had filled her eyes as she watched them both standing before Pastor Anthony exchanging their vows. They had both cried unashamedly during the ceremony.

Things had truly worked out for them all. Jerry had moved to Richmond and started working for their father at the car dealership. He had a whole new life and Melanie was so happy for him. He had come to know Christ as his savior in jail. Now he was attending church regularly and his future looked very promising. He and James came out to visit whenever they could. Melanie had a family again. She had Michael and his family but she also had her father and her brother

Autumn ended up going to UNC last fall. She was on the Dean's list. She had given her life to the Lord and had truly turned things around. She had a good relationship with her Aunt and she still came home for vacations and holidays. The teens she met in the youth group were still close friends of hers. Melanie was so proud of her.

God had truly given Melanie the desires of her heart. She remembered one of her favorite verses Psalm 37: *Trust in the Lord and do good, delight thyself also in the Lord and he shall give thee the desires of thy heart. Commit thy way to the Lord and he shall bring it to pass.*

God had given them a wonderful gift when he gave them such a strong love for one another. Today she had found out about another wonderful gift. She was pregnant with their first child. How blessed they both were.

Tonight she would take Michael for a walk on the beach and tell him about the baby. The very beach where they had their first real date had been the place that they chose for their wedding and now it would be the setting for sharing this wonderful news. Melanie's heart was so full right now that she felt tears start to fall down her face. Her plan to be a cat lady that lived by the sea had been accomplished. The really wonderful part was that she had been blessed with so much more than she had even asked or thought just as the Bible promises.

Life was good.

Printed in the United States
71815LV00002B/165

9 781424 162055